Margaret J. Carr's

THE WORLD ACCORDING TO …
OGDEN

The book is a comedy whodunit, a work of fiction and a figment of the author's fantastic imagination and opinions, so does not apologise if it offends the few who lack a sense of humour.

However, please note, no animals or humans were harmed in the writing of *The World According to OGDEN*

If any of the content resembles a real person or any actual events, it is a pure coincidence.

Margaret J Carr books ©2021

Chapter 1

He was cold and hungry but thankful he'd found the farm and the barn in which to spend the night. The farmer, he'd sussed earlier, lived alone in the rundown house right in the middle of loads of fields and open spaces. Himself, he wasn't too keen on all this nothingness, much preferring busy streets and lots of people and noise. He missed all that, but once he got to the next big city, 'hitching' or cadging a lift, far away from the past three years on the streets and having to live by using his wits, then everything would be alright.

He'd make sure of that. Get himself a roof over his head and, if not some sort of job, then get on Benefits.

The barn had been better than spending another night under a scratchy hedge with strange noises and wild animals all around him.

From this hiding place he'd 'clocked' the old bloke, who looked a miserable old git and seemed to talk and argue with himself. He was best not approached, but he might be able to sneak in later and see if there was any food hanging about. The previous day he'd been able to pinch a bar of chocolate and a soft drink from a shop when the owner had turned his back. It hadn't really helped this never-ending hunger which plagued his days and nights, and his stomach rumbled loudly just to remind him it needed food.

He'd heard these farmers lived and ate well, so he'd take his chances once he went and did whatever it was farmers did. He sat back into the warmth of the old, and smelly, bale of hay and waited.

He must have snoozed because he was suddenly alerted by the sound of a vehicle pulling up and stopping right outside the barn's door.

Oh shit. He'd been found out.

It was probably the cops coming to arrest him for being in the wrong place. Could he get away? Was there a way out the back of the barn?

He froze, unable to move as the sound of a car door opening and closing then, very clearly, the conversation between two men.

Not the police then.

He sat back and listened with growing interest.

Chapter 2

'It's a fair size piece of land,' Colin Watson, local businessman, property developer and entrepreneur, stood outside the large barn looking out towards the acres of farmland spread out in all directions.

'I should be able to get rows of executive four-bed detached houses over there and probably squeeze in as many as forty semis if I cut down the best part of the wood.'

He swung his arm taking in the ancient woodland known by the locals as Woodpecker Wood and, in a semicircle, he indicated a smaller field to his right.

'Over there would be a further block of low-cost flats,' he was getting more enthusiastic as he spoke and worked out the future plans in his head.

He chucked, 'It'll be like a small town when I've finished and it'll deffo mean bringing in more infrastructure, at least three more connecting roads not forgetting utilities, broadband connection---.'

The man at his side, less impressed, grunted a nondescript reply. 'Well, that's Ok *if* you get the planning permission. It's what they class as greenbelt --- but you already know that.'

'Don't you worry about any of that. There are ways and means of getting around all the paperwork.'

'Ah,' the farmer wasn't so sure. There were rules and regulations for just about anything these days including where you could build.

'Look Maynard, it's just a case of greasing the right palms. Leave that side of it to me,' said the confident developer, sounding as if he was explaining to someone with low intelligence.

'All you must concentrate on is how you'll spend all that lovely money,' he continued. 'I've already transferred a quarter of a mil into an off-shore account in your name to seal the deal. I've told you; you'll get the rest just as soon as my friend Councillor Fielding gets the go ahead from the planning committee, and that's a cert.

Then it's down to you and me crossing the 't's and dotting the 'i's on this prime real estate.'

Again, he waved his arm around the vast space.

'I can have most of the housing stock sold within a year. I'll build using cheaply priced materials, just within building regs', and sell the lot for a substantial profit, so you get a nice fat promised bonus, Denis Fielding then gets his cut, and everyone's happy.'

'It'll not be that easy,' Fred Maynard, in his sixties and living a solitary life on the farm, since his wife and kids had cleared out over ten years before, thought about the money now sitting in an offshore bank account. The thought of all that money was eye watering coming just when he was finding it hard keeping the farm going, what with subsidy cuts and new rules and regulations. What if this windfall, and such high and mighty plans, all came to nothing and he had to pay back the money?

'Easy? Who says life is ever easy, my friend?' answered Watson. 'What I say is, the good life is for the taking when I have someone like the Councillor in my pocket,' and tapped the side of his nose.

Chapter 3

Ok. So, it was a Monday morning and the start of another busy week.

The sun was attempting to pierce through thick, black clouds moved swiftly along by a near gale force wind. The weather person had solemnly forecast torrential rain with the possibility of the storm, named Clive or Clarice or something, (that's the storm not the weather person) arriving from the west sometime before nightfall. However, my trusted inner weather app informed me the next twelve hours would be sunny with a few scattered showers and a gentle breeze so, of course, I firmly believed my own personal prediction.

Saffron, my friend and housemate, had already left for work by eight thirty, heading to join the usual stream of traffic into the town centre and her responsible, yet highly enjoyable job.

I, on the other hand, having taken early retirement from my work now had the time to do what I liked to do best.

Nothing.

You would probably wonder why I'd not gone into more details and explanations about our chosen careers. Well, I didn't think it's a necessary inclusion to the story, having never understood the need to reveal professions like some form of badges of honour, and usually to complete strangers? It's as if what they did for a living defined their characters, their personalities, and their reason to exist.

Oh, for goodness sake.

So, at precisely eight thirty one, and left to my own devices, I pottered around and checked each corner of the small but adequately sized house for any discrepancies and at the same time managed to disturb, in one dark, forgotten corner, an indignant spider and a prettily festooned web.

Next, with the first of the rain battering the glass roof in the conservatory, it was a quick job watering the fading summer flowers and plants in the bijou garden.

Saffron had attached a reminder one-word note in large black marker-pen letters to the fridge.

BIN! (smiley face).

Another quick check that this important job had indeed been carried out and that the rubbish bin had been dragged to the front pavement for emptying later that morning.

All good, as to be expected.

The next, very important start to my day, was a hearty breakfast. This inevitably was followed by a contemplative sprawl on the long, extremely comfortable sofa, which always meant I had to share the space with our fat, incredibly lazy, cat called Tomski taking up more space than I considered necessary.

All my domestic tasks were completed, and it was not yet ten o'clock.

Happy days!

Chapter 4

The week had begun well for Jim Howard.

As always, his day started early and at first it had promised to stay dry yet windy, the weather he and his team always hoped for. But after competing only a small part of their allotted route, the heavens had opened making their job harder and infinitely wetter.

Married and a father of two, Jim was reasonably happy with his lot. Like with many young families, a mortgage, running two cars, a plethora of must-have techno gadgets and a week's holiday in Corfu each year, he would have liked more but he was hopeful he'd win the lottery one day.

But while he waited for 'his numbers to come up' he continued the important work emptying household waste and enjoying the camaraderie of his workmates. An early start was a bit of a bind, especially if he'd broken his golden rule of not staying up too late watching sport on Sky, but it had its good points and meant, if the gaffer worked out the timing well, they could be finished in plenty of time for Jim to collect his kids from school. With Elaine often working a late shift at the hospital, the couple could manage their time to fit in with the family, and Tyler's after-school cookery class and seven-year-old Brittany's football practice.

Gary was having his usual Monday morning moan. Gary's partner, Angie, was 'playing away', or that was how he saw it.

'She gets all tarted up, spends a fortune on getting hair extensions, fake nails and on a new outfit, just to go and spend Saturday evening with her so-called pals drinking bottles of Prosecco,' he placed the bin onto the mechanism, which would hoist it up and tip to empty into its cavernous mouth, and continued without pausing. 'Angie calls it a girl's night in. That's not what I'd call it meeting her fancy fella and then going back to his place. Who is she trying to kid?'

The gang had heard it all before.

'Angie is using me, making a fool of me when she knows how much I adored her.'

Of course as with every weekend, or it felt like it was that often to his mates, Angie would return home in the early hours, so drunk hardly able to walk from the cab's door to their own, having had a very enjoyable few hours in the company of her friends and giving her welcomed time from her over possessive boyfriend. This inevitably resulted in hours of rows, sulks, and reprimands from Gary, until the couple spent the entire Sunday making up.

The crew of Jim, young Toby and their gaffer Ted, would half listen without commenting knowing it was best to let Gary get it off his chest before they all moved on to the more interesting subjects of the qualifying matches played over the weekend.

With more than half the bins emptied in Morgan Street, he swore as the hoist jammed with the current half emptied bin. Behind him the others were already lining up bins from the neighbouring houses with Ted (aka Gaffatape, his nickname had stuck when early on in his promotion to crew leader, someone had misheard), confident his team worked like a well-oiled machine, so expected the bins to be emptied in line then returned to the front of the relevant houses. A jammed hoist didn't happen that often. One occasion when a household had crammed an old mattress, with pieces of smashed up table and an old TV into their bin, and had completely knackered the machinery, Gaffatape had been furious, making sure his boss, at the Municipal and Council Waste Management, had sent that particular house a warning letter and the possibility of court action if they did it again.

Gaffatape took control, easing Gary out of the way with a well-aimed elbow.

'Let me try,' he was short tempered this morning. His ulcer was playing up again, and this sort of time-wasting could seriously upset his schedule. He liked to be one of the first teams to have the bins emptied, the bin lorry disposed of its load at the landfill and back at the depot by mid-afternoon. Then home to a few hours tending his beloved and, possibly, prize-winning pumpkin. This year it promised to be a grand size, after months of treating it like a baby and almost ignoring his long-suffering wife.

He pushed the appropriate button and watched and listened as the mechanism creaked and groaned but refused to budge, leaving the half empty bin suspended half in and half out of the lorry.

'Damn and blast it, Gary,' Gaffatape tutted and gave the button a couple of hearty thumps: sometimes that worked if the working part needed extra encouragement. 'What have you done, now?'

'It weren't me, boss,' whined the hapless Gary, getting fed-up of being the one blamed for just about everything that went wrong.

Toby Lee, the youngest and latest addition to the crew, standing with a bin to be emptied next in line, yawned long and loud and leant an elbow on the bin's lid. He really didn't like these early starts, but he supposed, emptying bins was a job, something to do until he got a job as a DJ at a nightclub, and it kept his folks off his back. As long as he had a decent, honest job and kept his nose clean then they wouldn't go on about his cousin and how he'd let the family down.

'Well lad,' Gaffatape was instructing Toby who hadn't been listening.

'You get that side and help Gary. Jim and I'll get this side and see if we can force it.'

'There's something jammed in the hoist,' it was Toby who first spotted the guilty obstacle. He took a closer look.

'Looks like an old trainer's wedged between the metal arm and the mechanics. I'll see if I can pull it free.'

The young bin man reached up, grabbed hold of the trainer's heel, and pulled.

Weightier than expected it thumped to the ground at their feet.

'Yuk, it's disgusting,' Gary said. 'Looks like tomato sauce has been spilt around the top.'

Gaffatape sighed and rubbed at the sudden sharp pain in his side. Bloody ulcer. This find was sure to put the mockers on his carefully planned schedule.

'That's not sauce, lad. It's dried blood. There's someone's foot still inside.'

Chapter 5

I was just having a five-minute nap when Saffron returned home. My housemate is never one of life's quietest people and the whole house seemed to come alive with the sound of the front door opening, banging against the shoe cupboard against one wall in the hall, and the thud as her bag dropped to the floor before she made her appearance in the main room. I sensed she had not had a good day from the usual signs, so I opened one eye, gave a deep sigh, and waited to hear about her day.

'Hi Oggie,' she said. 'I've had a shitty day.'

Here I must pause as a recently heard and eminently suitable catchphrase sprang to mind

'A case of potty mouth'.

Now I'd like to make it quite clear, I'm not old fashioned in my views and I've even been known to cuss with the best at the appropriate time. It's just this modern need to use profanities with every sentence, on the TV, in the street, in everyday speech is, in my opinion, unnecessary and overdone.

Just saying!

Anyway, I waited to hear more, wondering what had upset my best friend and housemate to such an extent and if I read her attitude right, it had nothing to do with any time spent at a sewage farm or knee deep in manure. It had something to do with her job.

By the way I haven't said, but Saffron is DS Saffron Brook, that is Detective Sergeant Brook of the local police force, so her body language was probably to do with an ongoing investigation.

She threw herself on the sofa and kicked off her shoes.

'I've spent all day questioning a crew of waste operatives---.'

(A what?)

'They'd been emptying bins in Morgan Street ---.'

(Oh, bin men! That reminded me, our bin and the entire street of overflowing bins had not yet been emptied the last time I'd checked).

'--and they found a foot in a trainer,' she continued.

(A what?)

Settling herself more comfortably on the sofa next to the sprawling Tomski, who invariably took up most of the space with his fat body and bouffant of fur, she went into full explanation mode.

'That's right. A severed foot, in the trainer, was wedged in the bin lorry's lifting mechanism. It was a right shoe, specifically a size eleven, and---,' spoken as if to justify the description so far. '--- I would say male in origin.'

'So, no sign of the left foot or trainer?' I asked.

'The other half of this odd pair hasn't been found,' Saffron uncorked herself from the very end of the sofa, stood and disappeared into the kitchen where I heard her open the fridge, pour wine into a glass, close the fridge door and she walked back into the main room, sipping the wine.

With grace and aplomb, she dislodged Tomski giving just sufficient room to resume her seat and continued as if there hadn't been a necessary pause.

'Of course, the leader of the waste team, Ted Lovell, had the good sense to stop everything and phoned the police immediately. Dave ---.'

I'll stop the narrative right here to explain further. The Dave she's referring to is her immediate boss, Detective Inspector David Addison. Reputed to be a competent enough copper, youngish, in his early forties, good looking if someone with dark hair and chiselled chin is your taste. Married once, divorced with no children and it's quite obvious to a casual onlooker that he fancies the pants off Saffron. They have been known to have a drink or two in a bar close to the police station after work, and if their relationship has stretched to something more intimate, then I'd be the last to know.

I take it you will rightly assume; I don't like or trust him but that's my problem, and back to the story.

'Dave is to oversee the investigation and forensics took charge of the lorry, while I was tasked with questioning the four men.

Ted Lovell aka 'Gaffatape', I was told his nickname is based on the fact firstly he's their boss, Ted became 'tape' and apparently no matter what, they're stuck with him.

He gave me the routes they'd already emptied bins stretching over quite a wide area. As to be expected, by late morning it was a full lorry ready to go to the tip. There are four men in the team, apart from him, Jim Howard, Gary Bruce and newest member, Toby Lee. Toby is seventeen and a typical teenager and before anyone could stop him, had snapped as many mobile photos of the trainer and enclosed foot as he could. He's already flooded social media with this gruesome find and, to Dave's annoyance, it's gone viral. Not a great start to the investigation. Dave says all sorts of nutters will now come out of the woodwork and hamper the police's work.'

Dave says. Dave this, Dave that. I refrained from making a comment and Saffron continued.

'No one saw or heard anything out of the ordinary and, according to Lovell, it was just another Monday.'

'I take it, no other body parts have been found?' I asked.

'The lorry was thoroughly searched and apart from the expected household rubbish there was nothing unusual. The trainer, cheap, bought from a well-known store and sold by the millions. It was well-worn, the sole almost worn through, and grubby. The foot, dirty, calloused with advanced athletes' foot and the nails overlong. Early forensic said it had been severed post-mortem and a clean cut. With no hesitation marks it would have been a sharp knife and could indicate to someone in the butchery business. The initial findings are that it's a man's foot and probably belonging to someone, homeless or down on their luck.'

Saffron, stroking Tomski's ears, sighed and closed her eyes.

'There are no clues to who the owner of the foot is and, at the moment, no idea what happened to the rest of him.'

Chapter 6

Ted Lovell, known to his colleagues as Gaffatape, was more shaken by their gruesome discovery than he liked to admit.

The four sat hunched at a table in the canteen hardly acknowledging any of the other members of the waste disposal operative, quietly drinking their chosen beverages, except young Toby who slurped noisily from a can of high octane soft drink, and each ignoring the assemblance of food before them.

It was lunchtime and for the four their day of bin emptying had been cut short after giving their statements to the police. They were free to go, yet no one wanted to make the first move.

'Who do you think it is?' asked Gary for the umpteenth time, turning, as they all did, to their leader as if he was the font of all knowledge.

'How should I know?' and not needing to delve deeper into this unanswerable question,

Ted stirred the thick, black, builder's brew in his large tannin-stained mug.

'Poor bloke,' he said, wishing he was back home tenderly caring for his pumpkin, while Joan, his wife, would be baking batches of her famous Victoria sponge. Her cakes often won her first prize at the cake baking competitions, the same show he'd be entering his enormous marrow.

Instead he didn't want to be the first to leave although it had been a tough, stress-filled few hours and his ulcer was making its presence known.

'Well I think he was killed, and the killer cut up the body and he's probably in different bin bags all over the town,' added Jim Howard who hadn't touched his favourite blend of coffee or meat-free pie. He'd emptied his stomach of his breakfast, all over his boots and the temporary 'crime scene', seconds after the 'foot in trainer' had been found and decided he'd never want to eat or drink ever again. Even though married to a nurse, and Elaine would sometimes tell him of a patient's symptoms or injuries, this was different seeing it first-hand --- er foot.

'Probably--,' he muttered, colour had drained from his usually flushed face and was now the colour of the cream Formica tabletop.

'Well I think the cops could have told us more ---,' said Toby the least affected, and tucked into a slice of cold pizza,'--- as we found it in the first place. It seems only right we should be told what they know.'

'That was blood around the top,' stated Gary with a degree of morbid delight. Wait til he got home and told Angie. He could dine out on this for weeks and she might even show him more respect and attention. 'Dried blood,' he ended, rehearsing in his head the drama in retelling.

'Yeah,' Toby, 'I got a real, great close up of all the blood and gore,' he exaggerated before, already plugged in, he first took a large bite from the congealed food then turned up the deafening track on his phone.

Chapter 7

It had been three days since the discovery of the severed foot and I sensed Saffron, DI Addison and the investigation team had not got as far as they'd have liked. Of course, and to be expected, my friend gave me daily updates after work and I knew they were following every lead to see where it led, but progress was slow. This wasn't helped by the sudden notoriety that had come to our small town, thanks to the media attention.

The young binman, or waste operative, by the name of Toby Lee had flooded the worldwide media with the close-up photos of the gruesome find. This had very quickly spawned the attention of worldwide TV, radio, and newspaper outlets, plus quite a number of the curious, and was turning young Toby into a celebrity.

Of course, the curious, the hangers-on and the plain *nosy* seemed to be everywhere, filling the local hotels and bars, and even searching out anything that resembled a souvenir or keepsake.

Really??

This sudden, unexpected influx of tourism, especially coming as an extra boost in the latter part of the year, was not lost on the local dignitaries who secretly welcomed this sudden good fortune.

Even Councillor 'the good and great' (that's how he sees himself) Denis Fielding, was quick to attach himself to this back-slapping publicity by making sure he appeared on, or was being interviewed, by local media.

'That man gets everywhere,' stated a disgusted and unimpressed Saffron as yet another TV news outlet gave full screen to his fleshy nose, flabby chins and small piercing eyes, and sound to his forceful, overbearing voice.

'I'm the first to abhor this shocking find and the crime that has to have been perpetrated. But it has to be said this fair and historical town of ours, with its wonderful retail such as the well- known Starlight Accessories, not forgetting

the theatres, bars and nightlife, will not be brought down by this gruesome discovery,' Fielding boomed loudly into the microphone and I wondered if anyone wrote him a script or the spiel, issuing from his mouth, was all his own?

Saffron tucked her legs under her and reached for the drink on the side table, her eyes never left the man on the telly, adding.

'He goes on about the crime that's been committed, and wait for it, he'll have a sly dig at the lack of progress from the police.'

We both listened as Fielding expounded with:

'My fellow citizens rest assured the police have all the resources needed to solve this crime and, in time, our beloved town will be safe once again for you all and any future incomers.'

'Good God, the man's an absolute numpty. Does he ever think before he speaks such rubbish? Just saying that will scare our more vulnerable people.'

I could see my friend was riding her high horse over our illustrious townsperson.

'Firstly,' she counted off her fingers. 'As yet there is no evidence a crime has been committed, not while we are still questioning local and nationwide hospitals and mortuaries to see if a patient or a cadaver is missing any body parts. Second there are no Mispers reported, whose description might match up to the foot, and thirdly no sign of the rest of the body so no identity.'

She paused to take a long drink from the hot beverage.

'That man is a --- a.'

I could see she was having trouble thinking up a suitable title, so I helped her out.

'Moron?'

'--- parasite.'

Ok. I'd not thought of that, but it would fit.

'It's all self, self with Councillor Fielding.

He'd not be giving these interviews and getting himself on telly, if it wasn't doing his image and his bank balance a world of good. I see his good lady wife; Eve is not included although he did get in a mention of her store.'

I definitely had the sense she was not his number one fan, when Saffron declared, 'He's a dreadful man.'

Finishing with, 'He really is a first-class dickhead.'

Chapter 8

Eventually the fuss and publicity died down, with no real progress on the severed foot found in the trainer.

The report from the path lab stated the trainer was size eleven, the right foot, it was well-worn, over-ripe, grimy, and cheaply mass-made to retail in any well-known shop or store.

Conclusion, it was almost impossible to find when or where it had been sold, or by whom.

The foot belonged to a young male. Dirty with overlong toenails, calluses on the sole and a marked degree of athlete's foot but, unfortunately no other distinguishing marks. It had been a relatively clean separation, done post-mortem and with a couple of strokes from a very sharp, single edged knife, like a kitchen or butcher's knife.

There were signs and traces of dried blood on the severed foot and around the top of the trainer but no DNA match in the police data system.

So that was that and with no more clues, the town moved on and the fuss died down.

The media quickly found the next earth-shattering news to tell the world and the locals breathed a sigh of relief: glad to get their town and their lives back to normal. The gruesome discovery lost its appeal and was resigned to one of those strange unsolved mysteries, so beloved by some of the alternative TV stations while the story, an unsolved crime, disappeared inside the annals of the town's history.

After all, another piece of breaking news and controversy had quickly taken its place and filled the lives and minds of the town's population.

'Oggie, have you seen this?'

Detective Sergeant Saffron Brook, a top police person and my housemate, was doing three things at once. Multi-tasking, I think, is the correct title.

She was getting ready for work on the last minute as usual, seeking out her bag and car keys discarded the previous evening in various places around our communal living space after making a late appearance around half eleven (not that I was clockwatching, mind), eating a bowl of cereal and keeping an eye, and ear, on the local TV newscaster presently filled the room with her clear, if slightly nasally, tones.

'Well, not really,' I answered. I too was tucking into my breakfast so, with my mouth full it was possible she couldn't make out my words.

'As if we don't have enough to deal with,' Saffron expounded as the TV screen zoomed in on the group of people milling around a field with placards and determination etched on their faces and body language.

'I mean did we really need to have an early morning audience with that property developer Colin Watson. The man's determined to go ahead with plans to build rows of houses on the Maynard Farm fields which will include cutting down a lot of the ancient oak woodland, said my friend consigning the empty cereal dish to the sink already overflowing with unwashed pots.

'See,' she pointed at the screen, as if making sure I was still focused on the scene playing out.

'Look. already hundreds of protestors probably bused in from all over the place to try and stop the inevitable from happening.'

She muttered on, as she finally discovered her car keys and then started the morning search for her bag.

'Bloody hell. You know what that'll mean? Extra work for 'uniform' that's what, and there is already talk of bringing in reinforcements from the neighbouring forces.'

I understood Saffron's concern, but I was very much on the side of the 'Save Our Green Fields' and 'Protect the Ancient Woodland' on this, having enjoyed years of yomping across natural wildflower meadows and walks through the wonderful canopy of the native trees and rich, pungent scents of undergrowth in Woodpecker Woods.

That people like Watson and even farmer Fred Maynard, who had to take some of the responsibility, were prepared to destroy natural habitats and a major part of the ecosystem, and for profit, was unforgivable.

Ok. So, the previous and the present governments wanted homes for all. Very commendable. Everyone should have a roof over their heads, and somewhere to live, but with so many empty, derelict, and forgotten properties everywhere, couldn't they be put back into use before more destruction of Nature? I know I'm back on my favourite soapbox, but what happened to 'no building on the greenbelt'?

'The way I see it ---,' I began, giving my opinion on this controversial subject.

Saffron wasn't listening, peering closely at the closeup of the gathering crowd and the man standing back from the rest and carefully protected by three members of police.

Someone, very obliging I'm sure, had handed Watson a megaphone as if he needed help in raising his voice above the general melee and something inside me, a rebellious me, hoped someone had brought a few eggs in readiness.

There was an initial crackling and buzzing from the instrument before his voice boomed out over the heads of the others.

'People need housing and thanks to the Government's green light, this morning I will be handing in my vision to the Planning Committee, for at least sixty new homes to be built right here,' Colin Watson was buoyant and ignored the booing and shouts of 'shame' as he ploughed on to get his message across, not just to the protestors, but more importantly the news media now hanging on to his every word and nuance.

'Imagine it, houses for first-time buyers, growing families and retirement homes for the elderly in your community. This will not only provide much needed housing but will bring in jobs and investment ----.'

'And this has nothing to do with the millions you'll make destroying the countryside.' Someone in the crowd shouted and this was immediately added to, by more shouts and accusations from his fellow protestors.

'Everyone will benefit in the long run.' Watson bellowed, making sure his words drowned out the objectors.

We watched as, it was round about now, two eggs smashed and smeared down the front of his expensive coat and thick, yellow yoke dripped onto the toes of his expensive shoes.

'Good shot,' I shouted but Saffron just tutted and rolled her eyes. There were more shouting, cries and jeers from the protestors, as the police led the pelted man away in haste.

'Hey,' she said, bending to stroke Tomski's thick fur as the cat, returning from a dawn raid on the neighbourhood mice, entered through the door-flap and instinctively made for the waiting food in his bowl.

'Oggie if you've nothing else on, how about you and me take a run out to the woods when I get back this evening?'

Without waiting for my answer, she spoke the magic words to that modern all- singing-all-dancing accursed contraption on the work surface and the television screen immediately went blank.

'We could get closer to the action,' she mused without taking a breath.

'Ok,' I agreed.

'Good,' said my housemate. 'See you later,' and let herself out through the kitchen door.

Chapter 9

Like you, I mistakenly thought the 'run out' to 'get closer to the action', would mean driving the four miles to the edge of Maynard's farm.

Saffron had other plans.

'Now, don't sulk Oggie,' she scolded on her return later that day and after changing into her jogging gear. 'Exercise will do us both good. I've noticed you are getting quite plump 'round the beam.'

Plump around the beam???

I considered myself as slim and as stream-lined as I'd always been and I confess I'd been looking forward to going for a ride, but I suppose a slow and steady jog wouldn't do any harm.

The late afternoon air was clean and crisp, and there were piles of lovely, fallen leaves to scatter and I was really getting into my stride when we got to our destination.

Woodpecker Woods was so vast it was more of a forest in size, impossible to know where it began and ended. Where we ended up, the section of treeline which ran for quite a length smudging the boundary between the woods and Maynard's Farm and the place where the protestors were protesting, it was surprisingly quiet and orderly.

As for me. apart from being slightly out of breath, (I know, a serious lack of regular exercise) I'd quite enjoyed the run.

Saffron, with me at her side, slowed down as we got closer to the protestors, rubber-neckers, few police in hi-vis jackets and the odd TV camera-person still hanging about, possibly hoping for chaos to break out amongst the remaining crowd. It seemed since the morning's local breaking TV news story, and the hurried departure of the man at the heart of this fuss, the crowd and general interest had waned, and the shouts and insults were thin on the ground. However, there were quite a mixed bunch but mainly young, and a remembered sweet smell lingered in the air, an aroma I'd gotten used to during my former job.

As we approached a group of three people standing a short distance away from the main group, I heard Saffron groan. 'Oh 'struth.'

Front and centre was a familiar figure, with his fiery red hair and the signature over-large army coat that swamped his slight figure. What was immediately evident was the tucks of angry scarring covering one side of his face.

'Brownlow,' Saffron snapped, her eyes narrowing with mild annoyance. 'Now, why am I not surprised to see you've shown up here.'

The man grinned and the side of his face formed into white wrinkles, but he seemed unconcerned as he answered.

'Detective Sergeant Brook. It's nice to see you, too. I was forgetting this is your neck of the woods, no pun intended, are you here to protest?'

Without waiting for her answer, he turned to me waiting at her side.

'Hi Ogden. How are you keeping?'

'I'm well,' I answered. I found it was impossible not to stare at the poor man's face. Arthur Brownlow, also known as Shem, well-known eco-warrior, climate activist and protestor, and an unwilling lesser member of the aristocracy, had survived an arson attack on his caravan in his own woods a year before, but sadly had not come away completely unscathed.

'I'm forgetting my manners,' he turned to the woman standing just behind him. She was probably in her seventies and her body language spoke of not wanting to attract unnecessary attention, but still wanting to be part of this protest.

'You will know the best-selling fiction author?'

Saffron gave a slight nod towards her, never having heard of her and taking little interest in the elderly writer. I, in turn, tried to recall any titles of her books.

'Mrs Carr has come to show solidarity against the destruction of woods and natural habitats, ---.' Shem turned to the young man standing back and taking particular interest in an ancient oak tree that just happened to be growing in his immediate eyeline.

'-- and Joel Clifford is from my village of Lower Mulberry and is at university studying trees.'

Joel, too engrossed in examining the ravages on the bark, didn't acknowledge the introduction or add his voice to any ongoing argument.

DS Brook had a reason for wanting to be here and took a closer look at some of the footwear being worn. There were many trainers in many degrees of wear and even a pair of very unsuitable rubber flip-flops. The writer was wearing a pair of sensible boots and both Joel and Shem were wearing calf high boots with jeans tucked into the tops. She asked. 'Has anyone in your group mysteriously disappeared recently?'

Shem shook his head.

'I'm assuming you're referring to the mysterious severed foot inside a trainer?'

She nodded.

'No, we arrived together, and no one has left up to now. All present and correct.'

The police detective was not happy with his flippancy, so her next words were sharp.

'So, you're all here to cause as much chaos as you can get away with?'

He replied in the same vein.

'No Detective Sergeant. We came here to try and stop this badly planned housing development on farmland, wildflower meadows and the destruction of an ancient woodland before it's too late.'

Shem was getting into a full-blown speech and at the same time his voice rose in volume.

'We are here to legally protest against the likes of this developer, Watson and the farmer, who are only interested in making money without considering the consequences. Did you know that part of this new development will be built on land that floods, meaning all the proposed properties on the west side will inevitably be under water? It's criminal.'

A few others, hearing Shem's argument, gave cries of 'here, here' and 'quite right'.

The detective sergeant was growing impatient.

'You may be right, it's not for me to judge. A decision should be left in the hands of the council's planning committee. However ---.'

She pointed to the sturdy barrier of hedges and fencing separating Maynard's land from the woods; her voice rose to encompass the whole group.

'This is as far as you go, so don't think you are above the law,' she could be quite bossy when she put her mind to it. 'It's private property so don't trespass, or you'll be prosecuted. Yes. You have a right to legal protest but,' now she turned to face Shem. 'I mean it. Just don't go causing any trouble Brownlow.'

She sounded stern, doing her professional duty, but there was a kindly glint in her eye revealing their history. The woodsman and a certain young rookie constable went back a way to the year when, as part of the police line marshalling a noisy group of animal activists, Constable Brook had very nearly been crushed beneath a serge from the angry mob determined to smash down the railing around the animal testing lab. A less vocal, and non-violent member of the protestors had pulled the policewoman well away from danger, as the metal railings gave way under the combined weight. Since that day, ten years previously, Shem and Saffron had crossed paths more than once, always on opposite sides but always with a certain amount of good-natured banter.

I wasn't too sure that was the case right that moment.

The young man, I think his name was Joel, was explaining in intense detail and showing the damage already caused to the line of ancient trees on the edge of the woods to a couple of girls. They seemed to be more interested in snapping pictures on their mobiles, texting and suddenly collapsing into senseless and unwarranted giggles. None of this seemed to worry Joel Clifford a jot, as he continued to explain to anyone who'd listen, his concern regarding some strange markings on the tree's bark and was then scraping off samples he carefully transferred to a specimen jar secreted in his back-pack.

The girls, cloned and tattooed, took a couple of selfies with the unsuspecting Joel, pulling silly faces behind his back and more giggles, the reason for this merriment completely eluded me.

'Is she a cop, then?'

One of the 'warriors', a youth with long bleached dreadlocks and macabre black makeup resembling a skull, if anyone needed reminding that tomorrow would be Halloween, had peeled away from his own small group hovering around a very battered campervan, probably illegally parked in a small gap between overgrown brambles, and wandered over to see what was happening so close to the disputed land.

Before Shem or Saffron could answer, he yelled back over his shoulder to his mates.

'Hey, we have a plain-clothes spy right here.'

More of his skeleton-clothed friends moved forward with an air of aggression and intimidation.

I had been chatting to the author, Margaret, or I should correct that as the nice elderly person had been declaring her own fears for the planet to me. Seated on a collapsible, canvas Director's chair and sipping hot tea poured into a mug from a flask, she   pontificating her opinions of the state of the world, the incompetence of the world's leaders and what should be done about the looming climate catastrophe.

I declare she's a woman of my own heart.

'I think,' she had a way and voice which commanded attention. 'Instead of all this argy-bargy between the people in power, tit-for-tat and who's to blame,' she was very loud and very adamant, sweeping an arm wide taking in the scenery before her. 'The world should be planting more trees and not hacking down two-hundred-year-old oaks to make way for a runway.'

A runway?

Poor old soul I think she'd got the wrong end of the stick, but I didn't think I should correct her. Of course, I heartily agreed with her sentiment as trees had featured often in my life.

I never did find out any of the names or titles of her eclectic range of fiction but, on reflection, they would probably not have been of interest to me.

However, I did take an interest, and it also brought two of the policemen closer, as the four 'ghouls' moved, menacingly, in Saffron's direction. Any danger towards my friend and I was immediately alerted.

Saffron could look very fierce when she wanted to and faced the encroaching foe with, 'Back off,' squeezed out between her teeth.

Shem gave a slight nod and the four 'backed off' as did the two officers and I waited standing closer to see if there were any other dangers coming from a different direction.

Dropping her voice so only the immediate personnel could hear her, Saffron spoke.

'Look Shem, I know this sort of thing can get out of hand and someone could get hurt.'

The man looked faintly amused at her seriousness. Although slight in stature, he always managed to appear in command of his surroundings and people, and this was no different.

'I can promise you Saffron, no one here will suddenly attack without my say so.'

'Take this seriously or I'll be arresting you for ----,' she thought quickly. 'For affray, disturbing the peace and causing civil unrest.'

His damaged face broke into a broad grin. 'All of that? You missed out on public disorder.' He was just as suddenly serious again.

'I will make sure there are no unlawful acts perpetrated by anyone here --- I can't include your officers in that promise. Everyone here,' he glanced at the four who had wandered back towards the van. 'Will behave within the law as regards to honest protesting.'

'That's good to hear,' I sensed Saffron was calming down after her outburst. 'So please, make sure your people don't cause more trouble like throwing eggs. Everyone can and should protest peacefully.'

Even I doubted that would happen, I admired her sudden naivety.

'In any case it would be wasted now everyone's getting ready to leave,' he said as activists began wandering off. It was turning colder, and the wind was strengthening by the minute.

'I think any further fight should be aimed at the person at the heart of this proposed 'crime'. He's already had a taste of what's to come.'

'Who? The developer Colin Watson?' The DS's eyes narrowed once more. She knew how this could go, if carried to a more personal level.

'I'm warning you ---,' she began.

Shem slowly shook his head. 'DS Brook,' he interrupted. 'Believe me. This isn't over.'

Chapter 10

By the following day and probably because of a sudden, unexpected overnight storm from the east most of the protestors had departed, except for a couple of stragglers determined to wait it out in their dilapidated campervan.

Sadly, my second-best friend, Shem, along with his co-protestors had driven away and soon after Saffron and I were able to get a lift home by one of the obliging officers on duty. I could tell from her demeanour she was worried about something, but whether it was because of her run-in with the eco-warrior or the increasing mood of the different sides in this dispute or something more personal, a disagreement with her inspector? I couldn't tell.

Leading up to a final public meeting and with growing and stronger opinions on opposing sides the atmosphere amongst the town's people had grown toxic.

The NIMBY members of the community, as vocal as ever, were against any new-builds, and definitely not the size and number outlined in Colin Watson's plans, which meant rows and rows of boxes covering our beautiful countryside. And as many had grown up with and lived their lives in and around Woodpecker Woods, they were against seeing it disappear forever.

'SAVE WOODPECKER WOODS' and 'SAVE OUR GREEN SPACES' posters appeared on just about every lamp post overnight.

On the other hand, I could sympathise with the first-time buyers eager to have a place of their own and the young families, many living in cramped flats.

And there was the constant old chestnut from the business community of 'This will mean new jobs and prosperity for the town.' And so, there were just as many 'WE NEED NEW HOMES' posters being super glued to the walls and sides of public buildings.

Everyone had their opinion, views and, in some cases, agenda.

It was also noted, by the locals and anyone hoping to get his 'spin' on the proposal, that the farmer at the very centre of all this was keeping well out of sight. In fact, Fred Maynard hadn't shown his face since this had first become news.

I was in two minds about the whole thing and spent endless hours weighing up the two-sided argument. I may have stayed metaphorically 'perched on the fence' pondering and indecisive if something hadn't morbidly appeared in the early hours of 31st October and suddenly my attention changed.

It was the same nasally-spoken, local TV newsreader who broke the news around breakfast time, and my ears pricked up.

'When last month's investigation following the discovery of the severed foot in the trainer came to nothing, the authorities set any further enquiries aside,' she stated with a note of reproof.

'Well. It is now about to be reopened, after a second foot in a trainer has been found tied to a tree in Woodpecker Woods.'

I wasn't surprised that Saffron was already in the know and had left soon after, with 'that look' on her face. The expression which meant she was concerned, of course she was concerned with another potential crime related to the first, which had been set aside by her boss so the team could concentrate on a couple of lesser crimes, and the frown that spoke of her real frustration and anger that there was another victim out there. Knowing my friend, I just knew someone was about to 'cop it', and I wondered who would be in the 'firing line'.

(At this point I must apologise for my use of common phrases. It's just that they fit the current mood).

So, seriously, a second severed foot in a trainer? If it wasn't so serious it could be pantomime.

But this had nothing to do with a seasonal entertainment put on to amuse ----. Had it?

I had to think this out and settled myself down to a day of deep contemplation.

Chapter 11

She knew she was in for a bollocking, and frankly, she didn't care.

DI Dave Addison sat behind his desk and didn't speak for what seemed a long time, but in reality, was only a matter of a minute or so.

He stared at Saffron with an expression that told her he was far from satisfied with her recent attitude, and she now stood before him like an errant child in front of a Head. Her eyes narrowed and she continued to clench her jaws until her teeth ached, although her hands were clasped loosely behind her back, as she stared at the incongruous diagrams pinned to the wall behind his head. She waited for the inevitable outburst.

'I don't know what brought that on Sergeant, but don't you ever speak to me in front of the team like that again. Do you hear me?'

The inspector fiddled with the accumulation of stationary detritus on the top of his desk.

Saffron didn't answer. What would have been the point? He didn't expect a word from her until he'd had his say.

'What goes on between us when we are off duty is our business but that doesn't give you the right to ride roughshod over my investigation methods. Do you hear me?'

'Yes, I hear you ---- sir.'

He ignored her obvious insolent tone.

The sergeant didn't need to turn around and see the rest of the team trying not to show interest, and some delight, at what was going on through the other side of the glass door. Her telling-off was well-deserved and much overdue, in most of their opinions and her discomfort at, sensing their attitude, palpable.

'I said there was more to the first discovery and that we should have tried to find out more about the victim ----,' she said, her words tailing off as his mouth set in a straight, angry line.

'And I said at the time, we did all we could. There were more pressing crimes to investigate, not least the senseless vandalism at Starlight Accessories. As the store is owned by Councillor

Fielding's wife, it was decided by the *executive*, that it took precedence over a possible accident with no leads, and no signs of the rest of the body or victim. It's all about prioritising.'

DS Brook didn't comment but at the back of her mind she wondered how long their personal relationship would last. Dave Addison the man, was an attentive, amusing and very sexy man, but DI Addison the policeman was an overbearing, sycophantic, arrogant prat. She'd run out of descriptive nouns by then.

In her opinion, this whole sham of an investigation was sounding more and more like local politics and had little to do with honest police work.

'I still think that break-in was a convenient inside job. An insurance fraud most likely,' Saffron added, not caring anymore.

'And meanwhile a possible murder goes unsolved,' she paused wondering, by the grim expression on his face, if she this time she really had gone too far. Their current relationship was already on rocky ground.

'And once again the 'foot in trainer' images snapped by a mobile phone are plastered all over the internet,' said Saffron, her disgust evident in her body language.

'I know,' her boss and lover agreed, 'and they are making this into sick crowd entertainment by adding brain-numbingly, infantile straplines to their photos. They lend themselves very nicely to 'Take a load off your foot', 'Stand on your own one foot', or 'Dead on your foot'. All very amusing to a number of mindless idiots and I believe this particular trainer incident has been stage managed for that purpose.'

'What?'

He allowed a smile.

'Saffron, believe it or not I'm not a complete prat.'

So, he could read her mind.

'I'm beginning to think at least one or both incidents have something to do with the Woodpecker Woods and greenbelt land activists recently camped out there,' he stated with a certain satisfaction, 'and that should be our area of interest in the inquiry.'

Perhaps not! He was going down the easy route of detecting without any real proof.

'That is rubbish,' Saffron snapped, knowing she was pushing her luck with her boss. 'You want to make them the scapegoats.'

He swore.

'You should think before you speak,' he was angry. 'Why do you constantly disagree with everything I say?

She didn't answer but refusing to look at him, set her mouth in a straight line and stared once again at that irritating crime poster beyond his head.

'DS Brook,' he began. 'If you'd allowed me to get a word in before your outburst in there,' he nodded to the large incident room beyond his door. 'I was about to give the squad the latest update from Forensics. Now, because of your uncalled-for interruption you've set back my schedule and I have a meeting to attend in about ten minutes, then there's a press conference to update the media.'

Prat. Saffron didn't speak her thoughts aloud.

'I'll tell you their conclusion and you can pass it on. OK?' His subordinate nodded.

'First the trainer found tied to the tree is cleaner, better quality, size nine and another right foot. So, the only connection with the first 'foot in trainer' is the MO and I assumed this one is a 'copycat'.'

'What about ---?'

'Let me finish,' he snapped impatiently, reading from the screen on his desk.

'The foot, wide, swollen with a bunion to the big toe was, at least, two sizes larger. It had been forced inside the shoe and was the foot of an old woman, probably in her eighties.'

DS Brook was shocked.

'So, we have another murder, then sir?'

'Unlikely but not impossible,' he allowed a slight smile to transform his face.

Addison glanced at this watch and returned to the screen.

'Prior to the amputation, the old girl had been dead for nearly a week and kept in cold storage. Her severed foot showed signs of formaldehyde, meaning the body had been embalmed.'

'Meaning a funeral?' Suddenly DS Brook was interested once again.

'Yes, Sergeant. A good place to start, so get on it.'

Chapter 12

'Tell me Mr Pope, have you buried an old woman during the last week?'

Pope & Sons Undertakers was the third business to be questioned with just one more to go. The inquiries had been met with general derision from the town's morticians.

'Yes. of course,' answered an amused Gavin Pope, third generation of established undertakers. 'A few old men as well. Why do you ask?'

DS Saffron Brook was in no mood for flippancy. She'd had a telling off by her superior and orders to find out where the appendage had come from, and who it had belonged to.

She was silently fuming, as accompanied by the visibly smirking young, 'wet-behind-the-ears' Constable Lavers, she'd visited each in turn to be met with 'smart-alec' answers.

She waited for an answer and Pope, realising this was not a joke, was instantly serious.

'There have been funerals of two elderly females in the past ten days.' Gavin Pope, at his desk, scanned the files on his computer.

'Miss Emily Tasker aged eighty-eight on the twenty-six of October and Mrs Jane Morgan, seventy-nine years of age, two days ago.'

'Were both the bodies embalmed?' asked Brook.

Pope, continuing to look curious but refraining from asking more, answered.

'Not Emily Taker. It wasn't needed as it was a cremation. On the other hand, Jane Morgan had the full treatment, silk-lined coffin with brass handles and was buried in a family plot'

'An open casket, Mr Pope?'

'Well, yes. Her family wanted to say their final goodbyes, so it was left here overnight ready for the ceremony the next day.'

'And anyone could have had access to the coffin and body?'

'Well --- yes. Everyone working here.'

Gavin Pope, not sure where this was going, was looking decidedly uncomfortable.

'If you think there's been any improprieties, then let me tell you, we run a first-class business beyond reproach. Pope & Sons Undertakers have been in service to the people of this town going back generations, Sergeant.'

'I don't doubt it, Mr Pope, but you will have heard on the news about the severed feet--?' She didn't wait for an answer as the man seated before her had suddenly turned grey.

'We believe the latest find could have originated from somewhere like your mortuary. The foot could have been cut from a cadaver and pushed into a trainer before transferring to a tree branch ---.'

'I ---- I,' he was lost for words as the truth was slowly dawning.

'One of your staff could have taken the limb while the body was waiting for burial. That's a probability, isn't it?'

He nodded.

'Who had an opportunity?'

Chapter 13

I had thought long and hard about this mystery and with so much to think about it was making my head hurt.

The way I saw it, by the time my housemate returned we should be able to combine our intelligence and come up with some genius conclusions. Who knew, together we might just solve this strange case.

Without needing to ask I could tell, as soon as Saffron walked in the door, that she was in a foul mood and I guessed, rightly, the grumpiness, slamming of doors and kicking off shoes was all down to that *wanker*, Addison.

Here I make no apologies for using that word, but just occasionally only profanity fits the situation, and in this case, it was spot on.

She slumped down on the sofa in her usual place and before I could ask said, 'We have decided to keep our relationship purely professional from now on.'

She sounded decisive yet there was a sadness about my friend. I knew who she was talking about, of course, and part of me was pleased. I didn't comment, letting her get it off her chest.

'He's an infuriating arsehole, and never listens to anyone else's input ----.'

I let her continue in the same vein for a couple of minutes.

'I know you never liked Dave---,' she ended.

I didn't say a word and the room went silent. Not even the noisy rattle of the door flap and the huffy arrival of Tomski could break this atmosphere until, conscious I was changing the subject, asked.

'Any leeway on the latest 'foot in trainer'?'

'I've spent the day chasing my tail, excuse the pun Oggie, around the town's funeral homes,' she sulked. 'It was the boss's way of showing his superiority.'

Back to Addison. Saffron let it go!

I kept quiet knowing this next was important.

'The severed foot belonged to an elderly woman awaiting burial. It had been cut from the body and then pushed into the trainer.'

'Ahh,' I said, realising where this was going. 'A prank.'

'Yep', agreed my friend. 'I tracked it to Pope & Sons, the large funeral home on the high street. The son Leroy is being trained up in the art of embalming, so he can eventually join the family firm. Leroy Pope is also the bestie friend of Bobby Lee, who happens to be the cousin of Toby Lee--,' she paused waiting for the penny to drop.

'Toby Lee was the waste disposal operative who found the first 'foot in trainer',' I said.

'Exactly. Leroy was in the prime position to find another suitable foot, one that wouldn't be missed once the burial had taken place. Overnight he removed said foot from the body then, screwed down the coffin lid as he did after any viewing. His friend Bobby took it from there by finding a discarded trainer at the back of his cupboard, and cramming in the old woman's foot. The two took the objects and tied them to a tree, took photos and posted them online.

I've questioned the lads and Bobby said after the first incident went viral, they wanted to replicate his cousin's sudden popularity. They thought it was a great laugh when their postings had even more hits than the first.'

'A copycat?'

'Sort of,' she said. 'I could have charged them with wasting police time but from the look on their parent's faces, I think those two will not get off that easily. Bobby Lee's folks have him grounded forever, and it looks like Pope's are about to be sued by the family of the late Mrs Morgan for mutilating granny's dead body and then having to have the old dear dug up to double check.'

'But that doesn't solve the original gruesome find, it's owner or what happened to him?' I said.

'No. I've asked the lab to take another look at the shoe. I know having spent hours amongst the general muck in a bin lorry there may not be any real evidence, but it may be worth another look,' she sighed and rested her head back against the cushion. 'I think there's been a murder and we have yet to find the body.'

'I agree,' I said.

Chapter 14

'All I'm saying is, if this planning proposal doesn't go through, then I'm cooked.'

The two men sat talking in the Merc in the empty car park.

It was Councillor Fielding's car with Colin Watson's erratically parked sports car pulled up alongside.

Denis Fielding glanced unimpressed at the status symbol which had to have cost its owner at least twice the price of his own. It was so like the property developer to show off, from the car, a twin to his trophy wife Mandy's vehicle, to the architecturally planned and specially built, ultra-modern house, all glass and concrete with large gymnasium, steam room, Olympic sized indoor swimming pool spread over the entire below-ground level.

More showing off, a status symbol or, if Denis was feeling especially vexed or bad-tempered with the man or the world in general, saw it as a small-minded, 'mine is bigger than yours' syndrome.

The truth was, Denis Fielding couldn't stand the man in the seat beside him. He thought of Watson as a jumped-up nought, with no taste for the finer things in life. The difference between the bottles of foreign wine, stacked for all visitors to see in the Watson's ultra-modern kitchen the size of a football pitch, and Denis's preferred single malt Scotch. Two opposites and any other time would not have mixed in the same circles, Fielding a member of an exclusive golf club, while Watson liked nothing more than Friday's drinking with his old buddies until every man was legless, but the councillor, grudgingly, acknowledged for the moment it was wiser and more profitable to appear be the property developer's best friend.

The truth was Denis was a snob, old school and proud of it. He didn't mind if the town knew of his upbringing, only child of a single parent, basic state school education and an A-level in geography, he'd left school determined he would go far, make his own way in the world and he had.

Now he was head of town planning, but preparing to stand as the town's member of Parliament in the next election. He'd been married to the beautiful and elegant Eve, a successful businesswoman in her own right, for eight years and they lived in a substantial Georgian property filled to the rafters with carefully sourced antiques.

'Stop worrying,' said the councillor, already growing weary of his companion's mithering. 'You're not the only one with a lot to lose if this project is kicked out,' he paused, watching a plane fly overhead, and musing as to its destination. Once this was signed and sealed, he might take a holiday. The Maldives.

He and Eve had gone to the islands last year and found it very much to their liking, select, luxurious and very expensive. He was amused at Watson's choice of holiday, Spain, as being so predictable.

'Yes---well,' muttered Colin. 'Don't forget you owe me. I've already given you a hundred grand on the promise of getting the planning ---.'

'Yes. Yes,' Denis snapped. 'That's a drop in the ocean as far as Watson's Developers are concerned. Your company's rolling in spare cash.'

'That's all you know my friend. Unless I can show the banks and my investors that the large housing project is in the bag ---.'

He stopped talking wondering if he's gone too far. The less his co-conspirators, Fielding and the pig farmer Maynard knew about his precarious finances the better, but he was almost bankrupt, already overdrawn and the business and his future rested on that positive decision from the Planning Committee. His lifestyle was expensive, not least his wife's spending who, right now, was on a shopping spree, early Christmas shopping Mandy called it, with two friends in New York staying at a top hotel and spending his money like water.

He'd handed over the last of his loans, a mortgage taken out on his house, which he classed as a sensible move on his part.

The way he saw it, by giving Maynard an upfront payment for the land and fields surrounding his farm, he wouldn't be able to sell it to another developer, and surely a hand out, no questions asked, to the head of Town Planning would secure a done-deal?

Both men stayed silent for a few minutes, each with their own concerns and problems.

Colin Watson was carrying the weight of the world on his shoulders. If this project, which potentially was worth tens of millions, didn't materialise then he'd lose everything, his home, his business and even his wife wouldn't stay around for long, if her high-octane lifestyle was in jeopardy.

He was being constantly bombarded with Maynard on the phone and emails, as to when the plans would be finalised, and he would get the rest of his money? Now he wished he hadn't been so generous with the farmer in the first place: sensing Fred Maynard originally would have accepted half the money to secure the land deal.

It was all right Denis Fielding saying it was only a matter of time before the planning committee signed off on the housing estate: after all hadn't the Government and the PM constantly harped on about 'new homes need to be built'? Well, Watson Developers were ready to do its bit for the population and make a fortune doing it. The problem was it was all taking time and he needed to get things moving now, what with the climate activists all but camping on his door. He sighed deeply with growing frustration. It was all becoming too much for one man and he wondered how long it would be before his health suffered with all this stress? His own dad had died of a heart attack when not much older than he was now.

Thank goodness for the one person who could take his mind off all his problems. It was to be hoped the man seated beside him, never found out about their illicit affair.

'Stop whining,' Denis snapped, always short on patience and supremely confident everything would go his way.

He considered the title of Councillor Fielding was good for the time being, but Denis Fielding MP or even Sir Denis, then the House of Lords was even better. It was what he deserved, and nothing would stop him reaching his goal. 'You'll get the go ahead to build your new town and I'll get what I want.'

His eyes narrowed and two words sprang to his mind.

Bribery and corruption.

The pay-out must never come to light or his world, his dreams would come crashing down in an instance.

Quite unexpectedly, and making Colin Watson jump, Fielding grabbed the other man's lapels and brought his face so close to Colin's he could smell the sourness of the councillor's breath. 'Just remember,' he snarled. 'Never breathe a word about our little arrangement. Ever. Understand?'

Watson pulled his coat free from the man's hand. 'OK. OK. Keep your hair on. It's as much my secret as yours. Mum's the word--.'

'As long as you remember that,' said the councillor, not completely convinced of the developer's assurance.

Colin nodded his understanding, forgetting for the moment the argument he'd had with Mandy, on the morning of her departure, and the slip of the tongue in a moment of anger revealing more than he should.

He knew that now.

She'd been demanding and yet tearful when he'd explained why she'd have to curb her spending, at least for the time being. His wife was furious at the amount he'd said he'd handing over to Maynard and Fielding, and resentful to say the least.

'Are you mad, Col? Seriously? Two hundred grand to that pair of losers? Well I hope you know what you're doing, that's all I can say.'

He thought he did, but sincerely hoped that slip would not come back to haunt him.

Chapter 15

There were two things Eve Fielding loved most of all, and neither was Denis her husband.

In fact, she detested him.

He could be charming and attentive in the company of others he considered his equal but behind the elegant, closed doors of their museum-quality, much-envied home, he was an aggressive tyrant. All of his cruel, bullying ways she kept to herself because on balance Denis gave her the lifestyle she'd always craved.

Eve was prone to sudden ideas which would come and fill her world until they materialised. Like a child with the latest toy, in time she'd lose interest and find something else to occupy her needs. Some might say this was down to the fact she'd never had the baby she so desperately wanted, which in turn had been down to Denis's insistence a child was not ever going to be part of his life's scheme. However, if there was anything else Eve wanted, which ultimately fitted in with his nepotistic ways, then he'd consider it.

It was her 'generous' husband who indulged her latest dream, of owning her own business, and had subsequently financed the Starlight Accessories. It was Denis who chose the location, a large, empty property on the main thoroughfare in the town, and it was down to Eve's extravagance, it was filled with the luxury, highly priced household items mainly sold in the top class stores in the cities.

At first the store, Eve's very own project, was exciting and she delighted in employing staff to run it, while she went overseas to exotic destinations on never-ending buying trips. This was independence, a purpose and prestige and she had never been happier.

For a short time anyway.

Because she liked to spend money, and quickly decided, to actually earn it was a boring chore. The problem was, and it was a big problem, the councillor's wife soon lost interest in her new venture. Not surprisingly and not being a businesswoman, she left the day to day running to inexperienced staff so Starlight Accessories never actually made a profit, and this was made worse when the business account became Eve's own personal bank account. Being a compulsive shop-a-holic, meant the owner indulged her two real loves, designer handbags and shoes. She had so many Gucci, Chanel and other designer's shoes and handbags: most were still in their exclusive packaging and Eve had no idea of the amount or size of the collection which filled a room in their elegant Georgian mansion.

The councillor time filled with Council business kept his wife's latest hobby to the back of his mind until the strange break-in a few months before.

Although the alarms had been triggered, nothing it seemed had been stolen or disturbed, except for a couple of items in the bedding department.

This was a mystery to the police officer who attended the report of the fashionable store being burgled. There was hardly any damage, and, in fact, it was dismissed by the insurance company when it was decided no crime had been committed. It was the following day and avoiding any press interest, Eve Fielding went off on another far eastern buying.

Denis had his own suspicions and hired a private investigator who had soon proved him right. His wife didn't know he'd found her out and it was something he'd store away and use, to his advantage, when the time was right, just so long as it didn't become common knowledge or open gossip in the town and amongst his colleagues, he'd keep the details of his wife's sordid affair to himself.

But Councillor Fielding kept a close eye on his investment, treating the exclusive store as another status symbol, but even he could see it had turned out to be a bad idea. The temporary injection of cash, courtesy of Colin Watson, wouldn't last long but see the store through Christmas and he'd already set the wheels in motion to put it up for sale, as a going concern, in the new year.

Of course, once Eve knew she would object, with her customary sulky, pouting mood but Denis didn't care. His beautiful and elegant wife was only part of his public-image he'd successfully and skilfully built up over the years, but as always, she would fall in line and do as she was told.

Chapter 16

'D'you know what, Oggie? This is now getting serious.'

Saffron Brook, the best ever detective sergeant in the entire history of the local police force, (that was my opinion anyway), had arrived home looking worn out.

I have to say this, but since the final split between my best friend and her erstwhile detective inspector boyfriend, the 'infuriating arse-hole' (her words not mine) Dave Addison, she had been happier and not been quite so prone to sweeping mood swings.

But she did look as if she'd had a heavy day as she sprawled on the long, low sofa and sipped a glass of red. It helped her to unwind --- or so she told me.

'What is?' I asked, presumably the crime rate was getting worse in our small town.

'It's still six weeks off Christmas and yet everywhere is dripping in decorations and glitter.'

Oh, was that all?

Saffron, not really into the season's greeting, sipped her wine and continued looking more relaxed with every sip.

'I know we had a bad time last Christmas, what with the flu epidemic, but I do think some people go over the top with the celebrations.'

Well yes, I had to agree. In my opinion it was more to do with commerce and profits than a two-thousand-year-old birthday.

'I drove past the Starlight Accessories store on my way home. You remember I told you about their suspicious break-in months ago? The official line was the owner, Councillor Fielding's wife, had been in her office working late one evening and, not realising their boss was still inside, a member of staff had switched on the alarm. That may have suited the authorities and Fielding's group of cronies, but I didn't buy that for a minute. Anyhow, the place is now lit up like a cross between Disney's fairyland and the annual Blackpool Illuminations, and they've really gone to town with the big window display. Anyone going past couldn't miss it.'

Chapter 17

'What have you done?' Colin Watson felt a wave of despair spread over him as he stared out through the plate glass window of their ultra-modern architecturally designed house and onto the patio immediately beneath the window, the large hot-tub and designer, Alhambra-inspired garden beyond.

He didn't know the exact time in New York but from the laughter and loud music in the background he supposed it was late evening over there and Mandy was attending a party, possibly leading up to Thanksgiving in a couple of days' time.

'Now don't be like that, babe,' she was well practised at the cutsie, little-girl tone, knowing this would always bring Colin around to her way of thinking.

'I didn't mean to, but it sort of popped out. Janey was telling a group of friends how hard it was to get planning permission over there in England, and I said it depended on whether you knew the right people and could bung them a few hundred grand.'

Mandy paused, waiting for her husband to say something. When the line stayed ominously silent and hating silence, she continued in her wheedling ways.

'It's nothing babe. Honest. Janey just laughed, saying something about having the planning committee in one's pocket always oiled the right wheels. Or something like that.'

'I told you in confidence, Mandy. If it gets out, I could be in a lot of trouble ---.'

This day had started bad when another bundle of red final notice letters had arrived this morning. These were debts he couldn't pay until that huge building contract was signed and sealed and they'd be richer than he'd ever imagined. It had to happen and very soon.

She gave one her girly giggles. 'Of course it won't. I didn't even mention Denis Fielding or the farmer, or the two hundred thousand pounds ---.'

A denial from his wife meant the exact opposite.

'I'll make sure Janey knows it's a big secret --,' she corrected.

Oh God she was just making it worse.

'No. Don't do that. Don't say anything and perhaps it'll be forgotten --.'

'Of course it will, babe,' Mandy Watson said, hoping to sound positive but inside she was filled with uncertainty and dismay. She sensed she had said things she shouldn't, and she couldn't tell her husband the interest her revelation had really caused by the interested group. Mandy and Janey had been invited to a party by a couple they'd met by chance in the hotel bar. Now she was in a stranger's home, surrounded by people she didn't know, and she couldn't really say she was enjoying it. Her friend Janey always fitted in no matter what, but Mandy felt disconnected to their loud, raucous noise and the American sense of humour.

She changed the subject.

'We'll be back home by Sunday and everything will be back to normal,' Mandy sounded brighter, and Colin softened.

He'd had his moments and affairs, the most recent the fling with the wife of the councillor, but he did love his ditsy wife and was missing her. Eve Fielding's face and body, suddenly and unwanted, filled his thoughts. She was on one of her many buying trips, he'd not seen or heard from her for nearly a week and he pushed her image quickly from his mind

'Of course it will, love,' he assured Mandy. He was feeling guilty all of a sudden.

'Nothing to worry your lovely head about.'

Chapter 18

In the many shops, sales and online purchases in the town were building up nicely with the pre-Christmas rush and with Black Friday and Cyber Monday only a matter of days away. Yet all was not 'merry and bright' at the exclusive Starlight Accessories.

Previously Thomas Bamber had been the senior head of department at another major store. It had not been a too taxing position with just enough responsibility to play to his minor strengths, running the staff of two on '*Lighting*' and keeping an eye on sales and stock. His solitary, comfortable world outside of work, hardly any close friends, except for Nigel, and a house left him by his parents he shared with his cat, had suddenly changed overnight with the store's unexpected closure. Subsequently he'd been employed at the newly opened Starlight Accessories as head of '*Soft Furnishings*': in charge of cushions, throws, and the boutique designer bedding department.

Yes, it was a change of stock, and direction, but still a manageable size and, in Thomas's opinion, a worthwhile step up the ladder.

And it was gradually, overtime, and as the owner spent less and less time away, that more of the day to day running and responsibilities of the entire Starlight empire were heaped on the shoulders of the unfortunate man.

Oh yes, he had the experience and seniority, so Eve Fielding (if she even thought about it) felt she'd left the business in capable hands. It was left to him to cope with falling profits and the growing unease and frustration of the rest of the staff. Their futures and jobs were becoming more and more uncertain as, each season, the sales dropped off and every member of staff, from the stores early morning cleaning staff, through to the junior floor staff and the seasoned managerial seniors, were worried. Not least the acting manager in Eve Fielding's endless absences and, it seemed, all of the hassle that went with it.

Not that long ago, there was that unpleasant incident when Thomas had been accused of not making sure everyone had left the premises before locking up. The owner's husband had been especially angry, so infuriated by Thomas' negligence that the acting-manager had been indignant, and a little scared of the fury aimed at his head.

Of course, it had blown over without further repercussions, but Thomas still felt resentment and smarted at his unfair treatment. He had his own theory about that night which he kept to himself.

Now, when the Christmas stock was filling the store Thomas Bamber, was having another 'crisis'.

'The top floor stock room with the new, and very expensive Christmas decorations, is flooded,' he was informed by the temporary seasonal head of the expanded Christmas department. 'I would say most of the new stock of interior fairy lights is ruined --- could be dangerous --- electricity and water ---.'

Was it possible Ms Taylor, seconded from her usual position as head of *Homewares,* was actually enjoying Thomas' current dilemma?

The acting manager licked his lips and closed his eyes to give himself a moment to think.

'See what you can salvage, Ms Taylor,' he instructed, seeing but deciding to ignore the smirk which had set in on the young woman's face.

He sighed. The staff didn't care if the place burnt down and he was beginning to think he'd had enough.

What else could go wrong?

Chapter 19

Not far away from this interaction Monsieur Dion Chambeau formerly Stan Chambers, the head of *Design and Display*, previously known as 'the window dresser', listened and slowly shook his head.

Where were the standards of his youth when he'd been trained by the best in the business? In those days every member of the staff took pride in their store and stock, always ensuring the customer came first. Whereas nowadays, a new staff member stayed for a couple of days, decided the job wasn't for them if they couldn't text or email their friends whenever they wanted, and would leave.

Or that was how Monsieur Chambeau saw it?

Would the latest work experience, sixteen-year-old Lucy Evans, employed for over the busy Christmas period stay the course? Only time would tell.

Shrugging his thin shoulders, he switched off his musings, concentrating his attention on his own problems. He fingered the roll of red silk he was going to drape across the real sleigh filling most of the main window space. The material was quality, used in the high-end lingerie trade and not meant as part of a window decoration.

And the sleigh. It was far too big and, in his opinion, a complete waste of money. As it had been bought, no expense spared and, on a whim, by Madam Fielding before she'd left for her last overseas trip, he had to follow her extravagant wishes.

The allowance for his window displays was small enough, and she had squandered most of it on the sleigh and two life size fibreglass reindeers. (Thank goodness, she'd not decided on the full set).

He resented her interference, treating him like a junior. They were the likes of his current helper, Lucy Evans, useful for sweeping out the window floorspace, cleaning the windows and collecting items from the storeroom, while he should have been the thoughtful, inspirational, a creative, magical genius.

If only Madam F. had left the buying to him. Quite a lot of the window ornaments, the glitter and tinsel, which was only on display for a couple of months, he'd could have re-used from last year and he could have spent the display budget on originality, and quality.

Never mind. It wasn't to be!

He'd realised quickly, after being employed as the Starlight Accessories permanent head of design and display, that their boss had her own expensive ideas. He accepted this without arguments. His salary was good, better than his last employment, and the money she squandered wasn't his money.

It was Christmas and the season of goodwill to all and time to spend big, so what mattered most to Monsieur Dion Chambeau, were the retail items carefully placed in and amongst the display to attract the buying public inside the store.

He carefully put the roll of crimson silk to one side and picked up two large golden baubles. He intended to suspend them, with more of the red ones and a cluster of smaller silver coloured ornaments, along the back wall on his carefully made tinsel screen. His vision when the lighting was right, was it would then take on the image of a winter wonderland, with the hidden spotlights, highlighting the sleigh filled with brightly coloured softwares tumbling and spilling over the sides. This particular scene was Madam Fielding's wishes on her last directive. Although sleighs, reindeers and Santa Claus was a dated festive scene, and he'd have liked to update it with modern film-related characters, if it resembled last year's festive window, well, it was twelve months on and, in his jaded opinion, people had short memories.

He muttered to himself as he concentrated on his masterpiece. '*Poor quar* that *filly*?'

He'd never quite mastered the French language or accent, so his words were a mix of an English man attempting to sound like a native and a Delboy variation.

'Where is that girl?'

Lucy had excused herself with a loudly declared, 'I need a pee,' which had been shouted at his back, as he'd been straightening something to one side of the window. She'd disappeared for nearly twenty minutes and he rightly guessed it had been an excuse to Facetime her boyfriend. This seemed a necessary action at least four times an hour.

'Ah Lucy,' he spotted her hovering at the makeup counter and he pointedly ignored the rolling of her eyes.

'I need you to climb to the front of the window ---,' he indicated the specific place. 'Try and do it without destroying the display. Oui?'

Lucy Evans nodded and gave a disapproving sigh but followed his orders.

She wasn't the most careful of people, but he kept his patience as she clambered, without too much grace or care, into the long showcase window and made her way towards the front. The highly priced crystal vase, centre to a small side table, wobbled dangerously but stayed upright. As she fought her way to the front, he thought he'd seen his assistant stick out her tongue at a couple of young, giggling girls, around her own age, on the other side of the glass. This time he'd ignore her bad manners knowing if he reprimanded her it would only cause another unwanted strop, and it was unlikely those teenagers would have come inside to buy. Any potential sales weren't lost by her rudeness.

The expensive crystal vase shook and settled back down on the inlaid side table as Lucy pushed past.

'What is it you want me to do?' she yelled back to Monsieur, completely oblivious to the raised eyebrows, from a couple of the senior 'heads' on the floor.

'Just --- be careful. Make your way to the front. That's right ---. That bow shouldn't be there. I'll go and take a look from the outside. Stay where you are and I'll guide you,' Dion instructed.

He'd spotted it at the front, a large, very large, gold muslin bow was lodged against the glass and most definitely not part of his display.

It was chilly beyond the heavy front doors and the store's constant centre heating. He shivered, keen to see the offending decoration removed, so he could get inside and return to the warmth.

He mee-mowed through the glass at his assistant, exaggerating his pointing to what had no right in his Christmas display.

From his angle, there looked to be an object behind the bow wedging it against the glass, looking unsightly and uncreative and his expression was one of disgust.

Lucy took a long stride over a carefully placed collection of colourful stacking, storage boxes knocking them flying as she caught them with an ungainly limb.

'There --- there,' he pointed towards the bow as the girl reached and stooped to remove it.

Behind it, and hidden from the window gazers, was a woman's black leather, high-heeled shoe. It had been so placed it couldn't have been seen from any angle, until Lucy yanked aside the wire-stiffened gold glittery bow and retrieved the offending obstacle.

Even through the plate glass he heard her scream, as did the mulling window shoppers, the Starlight Accessories staff, its assortment of customers and acting manager Thomas Bamber, now on the verge of a break-down, all couldn't have missed Lucy's ear shredding screech. Customers and staff stopped what they were doing, watching in awe as the girl dropped the shoe, took steps backwards, tripping and falling over the crowded display in her haste to get out of the window.

Monsieur Chambeau swore in good old-fashioned Anglo-Saxon, then ran back indoors to join the general melee. He was in time to witness the one-off expensive crystal vase swaying on its ultra-delicate stemmed foot, toppling, and shattering into pieces between the legs of one of the fibreglass reindeer.

Chapter 20

It was midmorning outside the Starlight Accessories and the two officers were sitting in the car.

'Do you know what, Sergeant?' stated a concerned DI Dave Addison 'This is getting serious.'

It was almost an exact repeat, word for word, of Saffron's statement a couple of days ago but with not the same context.

The inspector and Saffron Brook had rushed to Starlight Accessories, with the rest of the forensic team, after the call had come in. Police tape was stretched across the path as it was an official crime scene, and the town central store would be closed until further notice.

'Three separate feet left in three types of shoes. Tell me, what the devil's going on?'

It was a rhetorical question and Saffron didn't speak. She didn't know any more than he did, plus there was still an atmosphere between them which should have been left outside working hours, and hadn't been.

The customers, who had been inside when the item was discovered plus the staff, all had to be questioned.

Inside his office the stunned Thomas Bamber sat stiff-backed behind his desk, hands clasped tightly until his knuckles were white. He was staring at nothing, in shock, his eyes hardly blinked and his only thought was a mantra of 'I must keep this together.'

He'd blinked rapidly when Detective Inspector Addison and DS Brook walked in.

'You are the manager, Thomas Bamber?' asked Addison as he took the seat opposite.

'Acting-manager--,' his words seemed to stick, and he noisily cleared his throat before continuing the sentence.

'--- I stand in whenever the owner Mrs Fielding, Councillor Fielding's wife, is away on a buying spree.'

He'd tried not to think about her reaction when she found out about Starlight Accessories latest disaster. She'd be sure to blame him. Mrs

Fielding always blamed him for every major or minor mishap. Perhaps he should give in his notice before she sacked him?

So, lost in his own world of misery Bamber almost missed the inspector's question.

'Where is she now?'

He'd blinked again to refocus on the officer's face.

'She left a week ago to fly to Singapore or Hong Kong ---.' He was flustered and wished his brain would catch up. 'I -- I can't remember where exactly, but she was going to the Far East to buy next year's stock. It's too late now for this season --- what with Christmas sales already in full swing,' he gave a nervous laugh.

'I don't know when or how that shoe got into the window; you should ask Dion he's responsible for the displays.

'Chambeau, the window dresser?'

'Mm,' he refrained from warning the policeman, Monsieur would not take too kindly to being given that title. 'Look Inspector, when can I reopen the store?'

DI Addison dismissed his enquiry with a sharp. 'This is a criminal investigation so the shop will stay closed until I say otherwise. I'll let you know. For the moment, while the forensic team does its work.'

He waved his hand in the direction of the sergeant.

'And my sergeant will take charge of questioning the customers and staff, starting with Dion Chambeau,' he glanced at his rapidly gathered notes, 'aka Stan Chambers and Santa's little helper ---,' the inspector smirked at his attempt at a joke. 'Er Lucy Evans, have to say for themselves.'

Numerous interviews later there was nothing that pointed to solving the crime.

Monsieur Chambeau had been nervous, then obstinate, then indignant about the gruesome find 'in my window display,' as if it had been some macabre joke aimed at him.

It would mean a whole new window display, after giving it a thorough cleaning: no blood or gore would ever be found again in his windows. It would be more expense, exceeding his window and interior budget, and how would Mrs Fielding take to that news? More work and no help as Lucy Evans, last seen dramatically running, screaming from the store, he doubted she'd be back. So, resurrecting the festive display would be down to him alone and with no additional help.

'Whose foot is it, anyway?' he asked the inspector, as if it was a personal insult. All attempts at a French accent forgotten.

Addison didn't give an answer, because until the severed female foot inside the shoe had been properly examined by the experts, he didn't have the answers.

He'd taken a quick look, before the limb had been rushed off to the lab. It had disturbed his evening meal of a curry, and his now fragile digestion. The image wasn't something he wanted to dwell on.

He sat in the car with his sergeant, as she read out details from her notes.

'It's a left and obviously female. Small size 6. The limb appeared to be clean and pampered, with no signs of corns or calluses, and the nails painted scarlet.'

Saffron continued to read out her notes in a monotone. Dave Addison could have found out all the details from the source, the head of forensics, if he'd asked. Instead he'd waited for the sergeant to relay the findings, and consequently wasted time.

She wanted to tell him to grow up but what was the point? She felt he was doing this on purpose making sure, now she'd dumped him, she remembered her place. How long could they continue to work together in this atmosphere? It was a question she often asked herself, yet already guessing at the final answer.

She continued without objecting or commenting.

'The wound just below the ankle bone, severing the foot from the leg, was not as clean a cut as the previous two. This time it indicates a hurried, amateur slicing and almost certainly done post-mortem.'

He listened.

'The shoe, with a three-inch stiletto heel colour midnight-blue is soft pigskin and from a top Italian designer.'

Here Saffron stopped reading from her notes to add.

'Investigations are ongoing as to the retailer and, apart from the obvious 'foot in footwear', at present there seems to be no other connections to the other two incidents.'

'So, no identification?'

'Not yet. We may have to wait on DNA and blood matches to know who the foot belongs to.'

DI Addison suddenly burped loudly expelling a cloud of stale curry into the car's interior. He didn't apologise and his sergeant wrinkled her nose in disgust, thankful it wasn't worse, and stated. 'Unless a body turns up, sir.'

Chapter 21

This really was a mystery. Even I, with all my years of intelligent investigating, could not make sense of it.

'You know what Oggie I feel like we're being played,' said Saffron giving me a daily update. 'The owner of the first foot in a trainer remains an unknown recipient and I've no confirmation of how it got into the bin lorry. I'm still waiting to hear back from the lab on the extra tests I asked for. Dave Addison will have a fit when he finds out about my unauthorised request, but what the hell ---?'

I was pleased to see her uncertainty over their break-up the last few days, now seemed resolved in her mind, and my friend was happier.

'The second foot was a daft prank by the Lee boys, helped by the undertaker's son, Leroy, and seems to have been a one-off. Their families were not happy about their actions and I don't think they'll be trying another trick like that one anytime soon.'

Saffron grinned. 'Although it would seem the 'Foot in Trainer' has made the three lads overnight media celebs.'

She took on a serious look again. 'I dread what would have happened if they'd been able to get a snapshot of the third. My arse-licking 'it's all about prioritizing and fucking politics' boss would have gone ape-shit.'

I ignored her flowery language because in my opinion 'her boss' deserved it, anyway she changed the subject, so I was pleased Saffron didn't dwell on Dave Addison and, hopefully, she had 'moved on' after all.

'So not a prank this time?' I asked.

'At first the window dresser, -- er Window and Interior Retail Designer or whatever, Monsieur Dion Chambreau thought it was one of those macabre stage props someone had placed in the window as a joke aimed at him. From my first impression of the man, a sense of humour is not top of his 'must have' list. It's a real woman's foot, in a very expensive shoe. It was discovered at the front of the Starlight Accessories window amongst the elaborate

Christmas display, hidden beneath one of those large, gaudy bows used for decoration. The young girl who found it, a temporary member of their Christmas staff, had to be tracked down by one of our female officers after she ran home and locked herself in her room.

Lucy Evans mother said her daughter had never had such a terrible fright, she was traumatised and may never recover from the shock, so the Evans will be suing Starlight Accessories in the new year for compensation, for the mental stress caused.

The acting manager, a very nervous Thomas Bamber, wasn't much help. He didn't know where Mrs Fielding was or when she was due back. Naturally denied all knowledge of the offending object, except to say it would probably have stayed there undiscovered until the festive window was dismantled on closing, on Christmas Eve to make way for the New Year Sale ---.'

'Or the item started to smell,' I added.

'It would have built up quite a pong over time,' Saffron agreed.

'As the store is owned by Councillor Fielding's wife, who is apparently abroad at the moment, we will have to speak to her husband. The DI was informed that the councillor was on important, official Council duty all day and unable to be contacted, so we had to make an appointment to see the great man in his office tomorrow.'

I remembered he was notoriously sharp tempered and had little time for anything other than self-interest, so how would he react to this unsavoury news however tenuous the connection?

'Well. Good luck with that,' I added.

The two CID officers were shown into the inner sanctum, well within the allotted time the next morning.

Seated behind a desk in a surprisingly modern office, he was talking on the phone. With a wave of his hand he indicated Addison and Brook should sit on the two chairs facing him, while he completed the call.

He was listening to the person on the other end with growing impatience by the frown between his brows and the straight set of his mouth. Wearing an expensive suit, tailored and bespoke to accommodate his spreading waistline, Fielding wasn't a big man in stature yet he managed to exude an image of one of importance. He drummed his fingers on the desktop as a sudden irritated response to the caller. 'Just get on with it and call me back when it's been finalised.' He slammed down the receiver with force. It was obvious he expected his word to be law.

Almost without taking a breath he addressed the man, dismissing Saffron, and automatically assuming Addison's superiority.

'Detective Inspector --,' he glanced at the note his secretary had left on his desk.

'Addison. What can I do for you?'

His thin, straight mouth, above his couple of chins, raised slightly at the corners, indicating his version of a smile.

'Always happy to help our wonderful police force.'

'Councillor Fielding I'm sorry to take up your valuable time and I'm sure this unfortunate matter has absolutely nothing to do with yourself or Mrs Fielding---?' Addison could be just as smarmy or diplomatic depending on your viewpoint.

'My secretary said it was a matter of importance and that you wanted to speak to me in person,' Fielding glanced at his watch, gold and large and obviously flashy. 'I can give you ten minutes, then I've got an important meeting.'

'Your flannel may impress others,' thought the sergeant completely ignored by both men. 'But it doesn't impress me.' Saffron was itching to wipe the supercilious smirk from the councillor's face and to tell her boss to get on with it.

'We believe Mrs Fielding is abroad on business, is that right?' asked the inspector. 'Have you heard from her since she left the country last week?'

'No,' he looked puzzled as if wondering where this was going. 'No, she never does when she's travelling, we are both busy people. What's this about?'

'Starlight Accessories is owned by your wife?' The inspector didn't wait for an answer. 'An item of interest has been discovered and, as from yesterday morning, the store is closed and being treated as a potential crime scene.'

'What item? Couldn't this have waited until Eve returned. I have very little to do with my wife's interests ---.' He paused and the smirk, pretending to be a man-to-man grin, returned.

'I like to think of the store as the 'little woman's' hobby, do you understand?'

Saffron rolled her eyes and fought down the desire to feint the act of retching.

'I'm sorry, but no this can't wait,' Dave Addison actually sounded like a detective inspector. 'This is a serious matter.'

He took his mobile from his pocket and rolled through the photos until he found the one to show the man seated opposite.

It was a side-on image of a woman's stiletto. It looked expensive but there was nothing to indicate it was anything other than the right one to a pair.

'Does your wife have a pair of shoes like this one?'

Councillor Fielding gave a deep sigh, a sign he was growing bored with this and wanted the two to leave him to the more important work of the Planning Committee.

He merely glanced at the photo and shook his head indicating uninterest.

'No. Definitely not and in any case, she'd never wear a shoe that colour. She always prefers strong colours, to match her bright outfits, but she'd never wear anything as dull as navy blue.'

'Are you sure Mrs Fielding hasn't a pair of shoes like that?'

A dark, reddish purple blush spread across his face, a sign he was losing his temper.

'I've just said that Inspector Addison,' he pulled himself forward from his previous relaxed position. 'Now, I don't know what this is about, but I have more pressing matters --- so if you wouldn't mind ---?'

Fielding stood and the two officers were shown out of his office.

Neither spoke, until they were clear of the Council building and once more seated in Brook's car.

'So,' she said, pulling out of the car park and into the heavy morning's traffic. 'What did you make of that?'

'That he's an overbearing prat.'

'Glad we agree on something,' mused his sergeant.

'I think it's odd he didn't ask what had been found that was serious enough to close his wife's business, or how it's connected to a potential crime. In fact, he wasn't interested in any of it,' Addison said.

'When I showed him the photo, he made light of it, indicating it couldn't possibly have belonged to his wife, but never once was he curious enough to ask more.'

'Well, I don't trust him,' said Saffron as they neared the police headquarters. 'The little woman's hobby', what century is he from?'

Dave ignored his sergeant's disgust at the councillor's sexist remark.

'I hope the lab has some news on any DNA,' he said. 'Hopefully we can then know who last wore the shoe.'

It was a day later when, 'There is no doubt about it,' Addison was reading the latest lab results on his screen. 'They were able to find traces on a hairbrush Eve Fielding kept in her locked desk in her office at Starlight Accessories. The DNA matches the blood found on the shoe. It's her blood and her shoe, and we are now looking for the rest of her.'

Chapter 22

His face was livid, his features so extended with fury that the veins in his neck positively throbbed.

'What is the meaning of this?'

Councillor Denis Fielding had jumped to his feet the moment the two officers had entered his office. 'I've been very accommodating over your questions so far ---.'Not quite accurate but DI Addison let that pass. 'This is the second time you've invaded my office and this time without getting prior permission.'

'Invaded' was a strong word, but again the inspector let that go. He was now on safer ground and it was time to make the councillor understand that this time the police were in charge.

'This really is too much,' Fielding blustered on and, although she had no sympathy for him, DS Brook hoped he wouldn't have a heart attack before he answered the relevant questions.

'I'll report this intrusion of my private and official office, to my Member of Parliament and the Chief Constable.'

Was he actually running out of steam?

'Heads will roll over this, Addison. Mark my words.'

Apparently not!

He plumped back down on his chair and glared at the two who, without asking, sat on the seats facing him.

'Councillor can you confirm your wife left the country on the 17th November?'

He was feeling peeved and bad tempered, but common-sense told Denis now was not the time to be obstructive.

'Yes --- yes I think it was that date, I'd have to check my diary.'

'I asked your secretary on the way in and he says your wife was booked on a plane to Singapore on that date.'

It seemed surprising that the man seated in the outer office knew more about Mrs Fielding's business plans than her own husband. Or perhaps not.

'And did you go with your wife to the airport to see her off?' A daft question he realised as soon as it had left his mouth, and from the amused expression on Fielding.

'Don't be ridiculous, Inspector. It was a business trip and not a holiday.'

He sat back swinging the chair slightly from side to side. At ease.

'If I recall that was the day, I had an important meeting with one of the country's major house building companies so the answer to your question is no. From what I can remember Eve had a taxi booked for six a.m. and I woke at my usual time of half seven, and she'd left the house by then.'

Suddenly realising he'd not asked the obvious, he leant forward resting both elbows on the desktop.

'What is this about, Inspector? All these questions about my wife. Like I said last time, if it's anything to do with her store, then you'll have to ask her when she returns.'

'And when do you expect that will be?'

'Oh I don't know. Tristram, my secretary, seems to have all the details of my wife's travel plans. Ask him.'

'I have, Councillor. He seems to think she had a return flight booked for two days ago. We checked and she wasn't on that flight.'

Fielding scratched his head thoughtfully.

'So, she changed her mind. Decided to stay in Singapore longer or go to some other country before coming home. She did that sometimes and without telling me, or my secretary, about her change of plans. Ok. I'm going to ask you for a final time, what is this about?'

'The picture of the shoe I showed you, it does belong to your wife. The DNA proves it. The shoe was found in the main window of Starlight Accessories. Do you have any ideas as to how it got there?'

'No. I'm guessing they were a pair she had in the shop and left them or forgot them. I suppose one got transferred to the window by mistake. I have no idea what happened in that place, or how my wife ran it.'

'You are referring to your wife in the past tense.'

'Oh for God Sake man, it's a figure of speech. Eve could have left a pair of shoes there and will wonder what she's done with them when she gets home.'

'We have reason to believe something happened to Mrs Fielding and she never left the country,' said Addison. 'We think your wife has been murdered.'

The councillor gasped and suddenly gripped his chest, as he dramatically slumped to the floor.

Chapter 23

'We all thought he'd had a cardiac arrest but, the hospital has assured him, his heart is sound and it was just a touch of indigestion. He's going to be fine,' Tristram Lang was able to tell the inspector when he inquired hours later.

'The doctors wanted him to stay in hospital the rest of the day, to be sure and do a few more tests, but Councillor Fielding has already left the hospital and is back in his office. It was a shock to hear the sad news of his wife but he has pressing business to attend to.'

'So our good councillor has priorities,' said Dave Addison scathingly. 'The important work of town planning precedes the murder of his wife, but that doesn't mean we haven't more questions for the man.'

Brook and Addison wasted no time in driving back to the council offices and, without an appointment, marched into Fielding's office.

He was seated behind the desk, looking none the worse after his health scare. The officers caught the end of his conversation to someone on the phone before he hastily cut the call.

He didn't appear to be worried about their return, in fact he actually appeared to welcome them.

'So, inspector -- sergeant take a seat. I thought I might see you again today and while I was being treated in hospital, I had time to think. It was a shock to hear Eve was dead and then the sudden pain in my chest---.'

He let the words drift, expecting empathy, and understanding from Addison and Brook.

'We're sorry for your loss,' the DI took his cue, then waited. Why did the man not show more concern? There was no real grief. For the dead woman's husband, it seemed it was business as usual.

'It was while I was getting over the initial shock, I remembered something that might be of interest and help find her killer.'

When neither spoke, he cleared his throat as if about to begin a speech.

'I have to be straight with you Addison, I haven't been exactly honest with you. I was embarrassed more than anything and I didn't want to ---- well air my dirty laundry in public, so to speak. The tableau press would just love to get their collective teeth into something like this, especially after the current untrue rumour about council sleaze. All fake news of course, but we all know the media.'

He actually smirked and Saffron was desperate to wipe that expression from his smug face.

'So, what is it you want to tell us but must be kept out of the public domain?'

She ignored the look of annoyance from the inspector at her interruption, but Fielding really was an overbearing prat to the nth degree.

'I'd suspected for some time that my wife was having an affair. I always knew there was something about that break in at Starlight Accessories that didn't ring true. I think the alarms were triggered by Eve opening the main door to let her lover in for an evening of sex. I

didn't confront her with my suspicions, I love ---
loved my wife and hoped it would all fizzle out.

She arranged to fly to Singapore, even
booking the flight and hotel so I had no reason to
doubt that she wasn't about to go on another of
her lengthy buying expeditions. It was that
evening she told me that instead of going abroad
on business in the morning, she was actually
leaving me for this other man. She refused to tell
me who he was, where they were going and said
she'd get in touch in time to arrange a divorce.'

Councillor Denis Fielding paused to make
sure the two facing him had fully understood
him so far.

'I told you what happened next. Eve drove
off in her car early the next morning before I
was up, and I've not seen or heard from her
since. Until you told me she was dead I'd fully
expected to see her back, deciding it had all been
a terrible mistake and begging me to take her
back. Which, incidentally, I would have done.'

Addison was way ahead. 'And you think
this man could have been responsible for your
wife's death?'

'Oh yes. A sex game gone wrong, or they had a row which turned violent, it all fits.'

'What do you make of that?' Addison and Brook were on the way back to the incident room.

'Well, I don't think he told us everything,' Dave replied. 'Selective memory or giving us just enough to send us off on tracking this lover.'

'Mm, who may or may not exist.'

'Did you hear any part of the phone conversation we interrupted?'

'He was definitely cosying up to someone on the other end,' said Saffron. 'Sounded like he was assuring the person on the other end that the planning was all but signed off and the new housing development was in the bag.'

'Probably he was talking about that expanse of farmland on the Maynard property and the destruction of Woodpecker Woods. Many of the locals and the activists won't like that,' he grinned across at her, but she was too busy negotiating the traffic. 'We'll be getting

more trouble from your eco friend, Sham --
Shem?'

When she didn't rise to his barb, he changed the subject. He missed their old, friendly, and often lovers verbal jostling, and somewhere inside he hoped they could renew their former intimacy, but right now it looked far from possible.

'I think we need to have another talk with Thomas Bamber ---.'

Saffron interrupted as she often did.

'The Starlight Accessories manager? You can't think Eve and he were--?' She tried to imagine the glamorous and beautiful Eve Fielding, falling for the nervous little man who seemed to have a permanent body odour problem. But stranger things happened in life.

'No. I don't think that, but I do think he might be in a position to have seen Eve with another man, if they kept their assignations to after hours and within the store, then he may have witnessed something.'

His place of work was to reopen next week, but for now Thomas Bamber was at home and nursing a bad cold.

He wasn't altogether happy at DI Addison and DS Brook turning up on his doorstep.

'I've told you all I can,' he argued, sniffing heavily into a large cotton handkerchief. 'But come in if you must and close the door, you're letting all the heat out.'

They followed the plaid dressing-gown clad man into a room which was cluttered with large pieces of furniture and heated to such an extent it was forming a fugue and hard to breath.

'I don't know what will happen at Starlight Accessories now Mrs Fielding has -- is no longer in charge,' he sniffed with building self-pity.

'For all I know, I could be out of a job in the new year.'

So, no sympathy for the dead woman there, then.

The officers didn't have an answer, so waited as he man-handled a cat off the one of two empty seats, the sofa, and sitting in a large, overstuffed chair beside a fierce log burner, indicated they should sit. Dave, not a great cat person, brushed off the remnants of fur and sat, while Saffron hovered, bending to stroke the cat's head and getting loudly purred at for her trouble.

'He's taken to you. Barry doesn't generally 'take' to strangers.'

That could have been admiration or simply begrudging Barry's new alliance? It was hard to tell through a sudden barrage of coughing and sneezing.

When he was calm again the inspector said, 'Just a couple more questions, Mr Bamber then we'll get out of your way.'

If it was meant to appease, well, the expression on the man's face said it hadn't.

Bamber blew long and noisily into the hanky and rested his head back against the chair back. Closing his eyes, he was a picture of martyrdom to the common cold.

'The night when there was supposed to have been a break in at the shop--?'

Bamber raised one lid and scrutinised the DI through a red rimmed eye.

'I did lock the doors before I set the alarms, as I always do before leaving,' he was instantly on the defence. 'Someone opened the door without thinking and set it all off.'

'I believe you, Mr Bamber, but I'm wondering if you might know who that person was?'

'I thought Mrs Fielding was using the store after hours to meet someone, but it was none of my business what she did, she was the boss.'

'Did you happen to see who this person was?'

A sudden light of cunning lightened his swollen, puffy eyes. 'Oh yes. It was that property developer. You know, the one hoping to build a house estate? Colin Watson?'

Chapter 24

'Well Oggie, that's the progress so far.'

Saffron had popped back home to collect her thick, furry fleece. The weather had turned cold within hours and the forecast was for snow later that night.

'It could be a long session if we can track down Colin Watson. It seems he may have gone to ground and it's a possible sign of his guilt. The wife Mandy is in the States until next week, and his foreman says Watson's not been at the site of one of their renovations for days. He tried contacting him and, when he couldn't get an answer, was about to go to Watson's house and check on things before we stopped him. It could turn out to be a crime scene. What d'you think?'

Now, you who know me, know I'm not one for poking my nose in. But, in my opinion, and based on the information so far, I would have said it was an open and shut case.

'He's guilty,' I offered. 'Obviously, or he wouldn't have done a runner. The way I see it,

Watson changed his mind about leaving his wife for Eve Fielding and she didn't like being dumped. They fought and Watson killed the councillor's wife. Because the act is 'of-the-moment', he then hacks off her foot leaving it in the store's window. Watson owns a building company and so has plenty of places to bury or dispose of a body. Then he scarpers.'

'Course, we don't know if he has cleared out yet,' said Saffron, grabbing a cereal snack from the cupboard and collecting her car keys, from their usual dumping place of the cracked dish on the cupboard.

'And if he is our number one suspect, we need to find him fast, so we, (I'm guessing 'we' included her recent love interest, the inspector) are heading to Watson's house.'

Saffron stooped, to plant a matey kiss on the top of my head. 'Be good, Oggie,' she added before heading out into the cold night.

The property, belonging to the Watson's, had so many security lights, all on elaborate timers, dotted around the outside of the house, and the immediate surrounding land, it was lit up like a Christmas tree.

However there seemed no sign of life and no one came to the door, when Dave Addison finally located the integrated bell to one side of the large pine door.

It was quiet, no noise or sound of traffic, but there was something --- a remote rushing sound somewhere in the distance. Addison decided to investigate around at the back of the square, concrete, and glass modernist building.

'You two wait here,' he instructed the two accompanying officers and Brook and Addison located the way through carefully clipped hedging to the rear.

The landscaped garden carefully lit by subtle hidden lighting in the trees and shrubs revealed a seating area towards the back. Closer to the large plate glass window, and running the length of the building, a patio was floodlit almost as bright as daylight.

A large hot tub bubbled away, the sound they'd heard from the front. Something floated to the surface then sank, swallowed up by the force of the water.

'Oh my God, that's ---.'

Chapter 25

'My best estimate is twenty-four hours,' offered the police surgeon. 'I'll know better when I get him on my table.' He straightened up to get a better look at the gruesome scene. Although the machine had been switched off soon after discovery, the steam from the water still rose and hovered like a cloud, clearly highlighted by the strong lighting.

'Because of the state of the body having been broiled over the time, it's impossible to say what the cause of death was without a closer look.'

Dr Jatinder Dosanjh, aka by his colleagues as Doc Jat, peered at the naked corpse. Now that all the photographs and preliminary examination *in situ* were over, he was being carefully transferred to the stretcher. The flesh was patchy the colour of putty and in places peeling from the bones.

The toes were wedged firmly in the dead man's mouth, so his large severed foot protruded like some bizarre comedy scene.

'I'm guessing Colin Watson's death wasn't accidental?'

The ME nodded. 'It's possible the hot tub's workings overheated, and he was first electrocuted, except --. As I know nothing about machinery or electrics of any sort,' the medic grinned. 'I have to call the experts in, if my electric toothbrush malfunctions so it's no good asking me.'

He was serious and thoughtful as he continued. 'But I very much doubt the victim first sliced off his own foot with that --,' he indicated the bloodied sharp kitchen knife retrieved from the ground, and now being placed in an evidence bag by one of his team. '-- and then stuffed the limb in his own mouth, just in time for the wiring to send a killer jolt through his body and cook him like a lobster,' his characteristic gallows humour made him add.

'It would be a case of dramatically overkill, don't you think?

When his attempt at lightening the scene was met by silence, he collected together the tools of his trade.

'Oh well, inspector, I'll let you know my findings as soon as I open him up. Should have a more accurate time and cause of death by midmorning.'

Doc Jat gave an involuntary shiver. The wind had strengthened, and a flurry of snow was beginning to coat the ground, as he followed the paramedics and the stretcher to the ambulance, and trudged back to his own car.

It had felt, just a few hours before that the murder of Eve Fielding was about to be solved as the facts had all fitted so neatly into a viable scenario.

'We're back to square one,' stated Addison during the morning's briefing.

'I think we should take another look at Councillor Fielding,' offered one of the team. 'He had a motive for killing both his wife and Watson.'

'Seems to fit, but we need more evidence. Has anyone checked his alibi for his wife's murder?' asked Addison, scanning the list and photos pinned to the white board on the squad room's wall. For the two murders, Eve Fielding and now Colin Watson's there was very little to go on, with names and photographs of victims and suspects, even less links. Some of the names had question marks beside them, with suspects with a connection to Eve Fielding, such as Lucy Evans, Dion Chambeau and the manager Thomas Bamber, could essentially be ruled out.

'In his first statement Fielding said he'd last seen his wife the night before she was allegedly flying abroad the following morning, he later changed that to, she was leaving him for the builder, Watson. The councillor's explanation for that change was that he was embarrassed to admit she'd left him for someone else,' said Saffron.

'I'm not sure I buy that,' said a voice from the rear of the room. PC Aden Wright, the young police recruit seconded from uniform for just this one case, had aspirations of getting out of uniform as soon as he could and joining this elite CID team, so it was up to him to make a good impression by voicing his opinion. It would make him look like someone who would easily fit in with the rest, and contribute to any investigations.

'I mean, doesn't lying in the first place, then covering up with what could be another lie---. I mean which of those could be the truth?' He knew he was waffling.

'Except we know Mrs Fielding had booked to go abroad and then cancelled her travel arrangements on her mobile,' said a thoughtful Addison.

'It could have been the reason her husband gave, that she was planning to run away with Watson, but with the disappearance of Eve, presumably murdered, and Watson's death we only have Denis Fielding's word for any of it.'

'Which puts him firmly in the frame.'

'What of the councillor's alibis?'

'The days following Eve's disappearance and right up to the discovery of the foot in shoe in the store's window, her husband has it pretty well covered. His PA, Tristram Lang, confirmed he was at meetings, council related works and attending planning committees. In the evenings he was out wining and dining in full view of others and, as far as we know, doing what he did whether his wife was home or not. Apparently, the couple lived separate lives with their own interests and jobs except if, as a couple, they were called on to attend important council dinners and public affairs. No one at Starlight Accessories saw him in or around the store during those relevant dates.

We know Councillor Fielding has had his own work-related problems and is possibly not as perfect as he'd want the public to think. Unconnected to our enquiries he's had to give a press conference recently, when overnight the news and social media broke the rumour of sleaze and accusing him of taking a back hander, in regard to that new housing estate planned on Maynard's land. He denied it of course, but it is being investigated. Thankfully, it's not our problem but that does place doubt on his honesty.'

The team listened to Addison with only a background sound of a few murmured voices.

The truth was, until Eve Fielding's body turned up, and unless a link could be proven with their main suspect now dead, murdered, they had very little to go on.

'OK we now have a murdered property developer.' He pointed at the recent addition of the photo of Colin Watson in better, happier times.

'The manner of his death, not forgetting the addition of the foot, it would seem *the feet in shoes* are symbolic in some way and there has to be a connection,' Addison paused, to make sure everyone was taking notice.

'I think both crimes have been committed by the same hand, but we'll wait on the results from Colin Watson's autopsy and take it from there,' he said, signalling the end of the morning's briefing. He still had the looming press conference, alongside the county's Assistant Chief Constable, to get through and called to reassure the panicked general public.

'There's nothing to worry about. These types of mutations and killings are incredibly rare.'

Basic 'police speak' from the ACC.

'Our highly trained police force is doing everything in it's power to keep our citizens safe and to apprehend the perpetrator or perpetrators in connection with, what the media is naming, 'The Foot Fetish Murders.' We expect an early arrest.'

Chapter 26

'We are getting nowhere with this case.'

Saffron, my bestie, looked worn out. She'd been up since early doors and it was now after ten in the evening.

'Dave thinks the disappearance and almost certain killing of Eve Fielding, and now the gruesome death of Colin Watson, were done by the same hand. I tend to agree with him.'

On principle, it was going against my philosophy to ever agree with anything the DI thought or said, but in this case, it made sense.

'Have you seen Watson's autopsy results?'

'As promised, Doc Jat emailed his findings,' she said, flopping down on the long, squashy-cushioned sofa beside me.

'Once the body had cooled from almost being boiled, bruising appeared around his arms and shoulders suggesting he'd been held down. He drowned before his foot was severed by a knife the perp found in the kitchen, and then stuffed in his mouth, toes first.'

'Someone quite strong then?' I concluded. 'A man?'

'The doc, without sounding too sexist in this case, is pretty sure it was a man. Watson was well built, and he would have struggled and fought his attacker, unless it was a powerful, female weight-trainer, ---.'

Her words faded and she closed her eyes. For a moment I thought she might have dozed off.

'You know Oggie,' she said suddenly, disturbing the peace and tranquillity, and making me jump. 'Watson's killer and presumably Eve Fielding's, went to the trouble of the added touch of the foot. We know both victims had had them removed after death, so that mutilation didn't make any difference to the actual killings except, in the Watson case, to waste precious time. He must have been very sure he wouldn't be caught out.'

Saffron was silent and thoughtful again for at least two minutes.

'The amputations were amateurish, almost hacked off, so that could indicate urgency.'

'Mmm,' said I. 'And making a point, or why not a hand, or an ear, or an eye?'

'Why bother to imitate the trainered foot on the bin lorry and then the media prank? Are they simply copycats and someone with a morbid sense of humour, or --,' she stopped the thinking-out-loud and again there was quiet, except when the cat arrived, in a flurry of indignant fur, demanding food?

'Ok Tomski,' Saffron struggled wearily to her feet to follow the swaying, fluffy tail into the kitchen where the feline stood staring expectantly at the food cupboard.

A few minutes later Saffron returned and took her usual place on the sofa.

'In the case of Colin Watson, the foot stuffed into the dead man's mouth pointed to 'foot in mouth'.

'Well -- yes,' I wasn't sure where she was going with this -- stating the obvious.

'When someone is said to have put their foot in their mouth, it means they've been speaking out of turn, or saying something they shouldn't, and most probably dropping someone 'in it'.'

'I see,' I said as the proverbial penny dropped.

'So it's more than likely it was a reference to something he'd let slip, and not necessarily following a pattern. And ---,' another thoughtful pause whilst brain waves reverberated.

'This, more so than Eve's foot, was personal. In other words, he'd truly pissed someone off. Which brings me back to Councillor Fielding. After apparently leaving him for Watson, disappears and her foot turns up on the premises she runs. Why? What's the meaning?

Watson is killed. We know the councillor and the property developer are pushing for planning permission to build a large housing estate, so there's a connection, but I don't get it yet. I know Denis Fielding's at the bottom of this but as for the actual murders he has alibis for just about everything, with hordes of people able to back them up, but ---.'

'What does your boss think?' I asked. I assumed the different scenarios had been discussed between the two senior officers.

She blew a snort of derision down her nose. 'My D.I, the 'I'm-always-right, so- don't-argue', David Charles Addison, has decided to look further afield for the killer. He's so up the Councillor's manipulative arse, he's decided any connection between the mighty man and the killings are nothing more than circumstantial with no real basis. He more less said the misunderstood, falsely-accused-of- corruption, Denis Fielding has become a scapegoat in the hunt for the true killer --- or I should say killers. Oh yes, if you listen to Addison, there's a band of eco-villains killing people and cutting off limbs, with Arthur Brownlow aka Shem at the front of the line.'

'Ridiculous.' It was my turn to snort down my nose in disgust.

'D'you know what, Oggie. He's becoming a right pain --- and more so now we've split up. He won't take no for an answer as far as that's concerned. I think it's all because I don't want us to get back together, in his mind we have to be in a constant state of disagreeing on everything. As my immediate boss, this is not working.'

She looked unhappy and uncertain and for the moment the murder case took second place to her worries. I could tell she was fighting an inner battle.

'Saffron,' I said. 'What do you want to do? Whatever you plan to do next, I'll be with you all the way.'

'I have a confession to make,' she took a long sighing breath before continuing.

'I've already put in for a transfer to another force.'

Saffron, my friend and housemate, didn't wait for me to comment.

'I'm already in line for promotion to detective inspector and it would have made matters worse between Dave and me,' she explained.

'So, I've decided it's time to move on. In the new year it'll be a fresh start.'

'Are we included?'

'Of course you and Tomski are coming too. I'm not leaving you guys behind.'

Chapter 27

Another morning's briefing from the detective inspector. He had pointedly ignored DS Brook, so she rightly guessed he knew already about her request for a transfer.

Well that was ok. He could be awkward and uncooperative, while she continued to do her job as his sergeant but maybe now, he was finally getting the message.

'The autopsy on Colin Watson tells us all we need to know. He was killed and a warning added for others to take note and not mess with the person or person's currently unknown.'

His gaze bypassed Saffron as he glanced from one officer to the next making sure each was hanging on his every word.

She just knew he was going down the same path and already was building up the case for the arrests of most of the recent climate and eco activists, who had been so disruptive and vocal in November. It would seem the possible killing of Eve Fielding was dismissed as a link for the time being, but could be included in any charges going forward.

'I want half of you to concentrate on putting together a watertight case against their leader Arthur Brownlow, who goes by the name of Shem. He's had convictions in the past for affray, criminal damage and causing riots at locations around the country, generally connected to some animal welfare groups or saving trees and the planet. He was front and centre when it came to objections aimed at the council and the builder, and the housing project in this town. He has every reason to get rid of Watson ---.' Addison stopped talking when the fresh-faced young recruit, PC Wright butted in.

'Sir, perhaps he killed Mrs Fielding by mistake and then tried to make it fit, by slicing off her foot?'

The DI smirked. 'Who knows?'

He continued as the young man beamed at the rest of the group, convinced Addison would remember him when it came to adding another detective to the team.

'The rest of you have the job of trawling through all the town centre and outlying CCTV and camera footage on the relevant dates. I want absolute proof that those troublemakers were in the areas close to Starlight Accessories on the nights in question, then again in the streets around Colin Watson's house on the days leading up to the discovery of his body.'

One last glance around then: 'Right you know what to do. Get to it.'

There was hours of footage to go through, both tedious and boring, and it appeared Saffron, alongside with the eager Aden Wright at her side, had been included as part of that particular team.

Pinned to the white board at the front of the Incident Room, so everyone had a clear view, an additional group of suspects had been added. The range of people, young and old, chatting, socialising and many yelling in one direction across the field, had been surreptitiously snapped and obviously taken on the day of the Woodpecker Woods/Maynard Farm protest. The very centre of the images was an enlarged picture of Arthur Brownlow, taken unawares while he was chatting to a group of Halloween dressed young people.

DI Addison, during his earlier briefing had made it quite plain, Brownlow was 'a person of interest' and finding him, in the locations on the days mentioned, was top priority.

Saffron didn't believe it. There was no evidence against Shem or anyone on the protests and she decided it was Addison looking for a suitable scapegoat. It made her equally determined to find out the real killer and she concentrated on searching the hours of footage. It was her eager co-worker Wright who drew her attention to the car.

'Sarg, it's the same vehicle in both vicinities on the right days and times,' he was excited by the find.

'See,' he pointed to the screen. 'It's the same make.'

The DS was more cautious and slowed down the footage to confirm the findings.

The images were clear: a dark coloured, unremarkable hatchback and late evening, with few cars using this particular back road behind the Starlight Accessories. This entrance was more often used for day time deliveries to the rear of the surrounding retailers but with the build up to the Christmas rush, there could have been a legitimate reason for any business or shop owner to be there at that time of night.

The street lighting wasn't good but clear enough to highlight a partial number plate and show the driver, the sole occupant, get out and hurry towards the rear entrance of Starlight Accessories. Carrying a parcel wrapped in what appeared to be a plastic bag, the person quickly disappeared out of sight.

'Someone in the wrong place and time. Fast forward,' Saffron said.

This could have been innocent and unconnected to anything of importance, but she sensed this was a significant find.

It was twenty minutes before the person reappeared, empty handed, ran back to the car and drove off.

'That was two days before Eve Fielding's foot was discovered in the window,' she said, excitement growing and affecting the constable seated beside her.

'Go on, Aden, where and when did you pick up that car again?' she instructed.

'Sarg,' delighted PC Wright, feeling he was at the very heart of this investigation, set the recording on to the next important image.

This time it was spotted mid-morning, travelling down the same road leading to the large, modernist Watson property. Unfortunately, it was a main road in and out of the town, so seeing any car on that road was not so unusual, except for the date and the subsequent murder.

Was it only a coincidence?

'Nice one, Aden,' Saffron praised the young copper. 'We may not have found it without you. Praise where praise is due,' she added as the impressionable and delighted young copper wallowed in the glory.

Chapter 28

'Exactly, why am I here?'

It had been only a matter of hours before the suspect had been arrested and brought in for questioning, starting as amused confusion and denial, but quickly leading to angry bluster.

'You are here to answer some questions,' DI Addison replied, seated across the table from the two people in the Interview Room.

'Can you explain why you drove to the rear of Starlight Accessories, at that time, on that evening?'

He showed the suspect and his brief, the clear photo images of the car and the person highlighted by the street lighting.

'I was on business.'

'Yet the store has nothing to do with you.'

A change of mood, from curious to sudden lack of interest, and a change of tack.

'I was doing someone a favour, OK? I was asked to drop something off for Eve.'

'What? What was so urgent it had to be 'dropped off' in the middle of the night and couldn't have waited until the morning?'

A shrug in way of an explanation.

The inspector also changed tack.

'What were you doing on that major road, on that day travelling away from the town centre and the council offices? I know it was a working day and that there was an extraordinary meeting of the planning committee that day, so how was it you were driving away from your place of work?'

'I don't have to explain my actions to you, Detective Inspector,' sudden indignation. 'You have no reason to keep me here,' followed a quick glance at the solicitor to confirm.

'I have every reason to keep you here, and following the evidence found in the boot of your car, I am charging you, Tristram Lang, personal assistant and private secretary to Councillor Denis Fielding, with the murders of Eve Fielding and Colin Watson.'

A quick word with his solicitor and the man confessed everything.

Tristram Lang, fifty-three, was heavily built and very strong, down to a strict regime of workouts and bodybuilding. His organisational and multitasking skills had meant he worked for a number of businesses, and organisations, before becoming the PA to the councillor. He lived alone and, when not working and organising Fielding's day, spent his free time at the gym and in a number of gay bars and clubs in the town.

All this information DS Saffron had found on Lang's Facebook page.

'Was Councillor Fielding involved?'

'Leave Denis out of it,' he insisted. 'He's had nothing to do with any of this.'

'So tell me who has?'

The man sat back against the chair, crossed his arms, and stared the inspector in the eyes.

'It was down to me. Ok? I killed them both. OK? She was no good for Denis, he deserves better than a scheming, conniving bitch like Eve. He said he'd agree a divorce sometime in the future so we could openly be together, but for the moment it was all about his image. He's seen as a successful man, happily married to an equally successful and elegant businesswoman and it fitted in with how the public saw him. He's very ambitious and he wanted more. He planned to stand as the town's MP, in the next election, and go on to be picked for a major role in the next Government.'

He paused, then continued.

'Denis suspected Eve was having an affair, he was alright with that. They lived separate lives, but when she said she was leaving him, he phoned me.' A tender smile flooded his face.

'He's so trusting,' his own impression of the man, wasn't quite the same as the DI listening intently to this statement who silently dismissed it as 'Love-blindness.'

'Eve threatened to tell the papers about his true sexuality and, although times have changed, her betrayal could have affected his future plans. I made up my mind that when she was leaving the house the next morning, I'd follow her and try to make her see reason. He didn't deserve her vindictiveness.'

The other's in the room listened without comment, the only sound the recording machine taking in every word of a confession.

'It was still dark and there was hardly any traffic at that time. I followed her into the countryside and flashed my lights until, recognizing my car, she pulled off the road.

Eve waited for me to drive up behind and then we got out of our cars. Of course, she didn't fear me, I was Tristram, her husband's faithful PA and secret lover. I tried to reason with her explaining how she must consider Denis and his career and that if she went to the press it could be the end of everything. She laughed, calling me stupid and saying things like, 'Nothing could touch my perfect husband,' and 'No one cares anymore which side you're on.' She didn't understand and wouldn't listen to anything, and I saw red.'

Lang hesitated and the people in the room waited.

'I don't know how it happened or who was the most shocked, when I suddenly had my hands around her throat, squeezing.'

He looked at a single mark on the tabletop, mesmerised by the shape of the coffee stain.

'Up until then, I'd not known how easy it was to kill someone, and with very little effort.'

It was then he appeared to relax, as if in the telling it had released all tension.

'What did you do next?' asked DS Brook.

Lang stared at her as if, just for a split second, he'd forgotten where he was.

He cleared his throat and continued.

'It was still dark enough for me to put her in her boot and I hid the car behind some dilapidated farm buildings. I thought it would be undetected until I decided what to do. I thought about confessing to Denis, but he had so much on his plate that it was up to me to clean up the mess. I got back into my car and drove straight to the office. Councillor Fielding had an important meeting later that morning and I was needed to prepare his speech.'

'So when did you decide to get rid of the car and mutilate the body?' Addison asked.

'Well,' the killer leant forward to rest his arms along the desk. 'As long as no one spotted the car I could take my time. You see, the Starlight Accessories manager assumed Eve was abroad and Denis thought she'd gone off with Warson, so she wouldn't be missed for a while. That gave me time to work out a plan,' he glanced nervously at his solicitor. Was he only now realising the severity of his crime?

'I was still wondering what to do next, get rid of the car and — and the body, when a chance meeting gave me the answer.

Someone who visits the same clubs as

I,' he didn't clarify, but the others in the room understood.

'Don isn't a close friend, he's not my type, but I knew he was the foreman on Watson's building site. Anyway, this evening we got chatting and he mentioned that in a couple of days there would be truckloads of cement for the foundations. He went on about it needing to be deep, because of building on a high-water table. I wasn't really listening too hard as he went into the details, something about the legality but as it was one of Colin Watson's projects, and his boss wasn't bothered about cutting corners.

Knowing the day and the time, and hours before the arrival of the cement lorries I first dismantled Eve's car, which I later left scattered around a scrap metal yard. With her body in my boot I drove to the building site, it was still too early for the men to arrive. I chose a plot away from the rest, and dropped the body, wrapped in bubble wrap, into the prepared space. Once the cement had been poured Eve Fielding would never be found under all that.'

He ended with a sigh of satisfaction: a job well done and no remorse on his part.

'Why the foot?'

Lang sighed.

'That was a foolish act, a moment of madness, but I was so angry at the way she'd treated Denis. So – after all the recent fuss about feet in shoes, I thought I'd add my own work of art. I sliced off her foot. Because she had used not only her husband's position but his money to pay for her new hobby, I thought it only rough justice to leave part of her in the window. I wrapped the foot and shoe in a plastic bag and the rest you know from the CCTV.'

The man's resentment and jealousy, but also his obvious delight, was almost palpable in the small, closed room.

Chapter 29

'Why Colin Watson?'

There had been a break and the four were now back in the Interview Room. If anything, Tristram Lang, having pleaded guilty to one murder, was calm and unconcerned, and not ready to take any instructions from his solicitor at his side.

The accused ignored DI Addison's first question and asked his own. 'When can I see Denis?'

'You can't. Now tell us about Watson?'

Lang was suddenly adamant and aggressive. 'But I want to speak to Councillor Fielding and explain how I did it all for him.'

The inspector wasn't about to tell him that the councillor was having problems of his own, currently under police investigation for corruption and accepting bribes. He had already distanced himself from his PA's activities and Tristram Lang had been 'thrown under the bus'!

'Councillor Fielding, as I'm sure you'll agree, is a busy man?'

Lang nodded, and concentrated once more on the coffee stain with an expression of petulance and acceptance, puckered around his fleshy mouth.

'Why kill Watson?' Addison repeated his earlier questions.

'He couldn't keep his mouth shut. He had to blab to that slutty wife of his.'

'Ah,' the DI said. 'Foot in mouth.'

'Mm,' Lang unconsciously scratched at the stain with a nail and nodded.

'He let slip to Mandy, about his backhanders to Denis and Maynard. They were hefty down-payments to ensure he got both the land from the farmer, and the council's planning permission to build, what would be the size of a small town, on the greenbelt land.

Just like her husband, she couldn't keep her mouth shut and told someone in the States who thought it would be amusing to post the details on the internet. Bloody social media. Nothing's sacred anymore.'

'Then,' he continued. 'When a major construction company put in their bid to build new houses, and with a better offer, Denis and the planning committee were ready to go with that one. Colin Watson was, understandable, miffed and threatened to go to the papers if he wasn't given the contract. He was about to blackmail Denis if he didn't get his own way.'

'And once again you had to make it right for your lover?'

'Yeah. I've always put things right. I don't know what I meant to do when I drove to Watson's house. I suppose I hoped to argue or plead with the man, to make him see sense.'

He listened to something whispered by the solicitor, but waved his hand indicating he would not issue the usual 'No comment' to the rest of the questions. Tristram Lang wanted to bare his soul with no thought to the inevitable consequences.

'He was in the hot tub when you found him?'

'I rang the doorbell of that awful building he'd had designed for himself by an architect who could only have been high on drugs at the time,' he was disgusted. 'You should have heard what Denis thought of that house. He said it resembled a utilitarian air-raid shelter built during the war, it was that grotesque. We laughed at the sheer audacity of Colin Watson, that he thought it made him an important part of the establishment and with that house he somehow fitted in. Watson and his small-scale building firm is what it is —'. His scorn fizzled out and it seemed he'd nothing more to add.

'So you found him in the hot tub at the back of the house?' asked the sergeant.

Lang glanced up at her and sighed.

'I hadn't gone to kill him'

'But you did –.'

'I'd gone to reason with him, but he thought it was all a big joke and that he had Denis, and the planning committee, over a barrel. There was no way anyone was going to turn him down, not with what he knew, and I couldn't let that happen,' he hesitated, nervously running his tongue around his lips.

'It was surprisingly straightforward to take him off guard and strangle him,' he admitted quietly.

'Watson was unfit, flabby and I found his nakedness repulsive. Once he was dead, floating amongst the bubbling, hot water streams, I thought shoving his foot in his mouth was pay back. He even had a conveniently extra sharp knife in his kitchen drawer. Once the foot was in the right place,' he grinned. 'I did think of shoving it up his –- well, never mind. Anyhow I reset the thermostat on the hot tub to very hot, just to indicate his indiscretion had landed him in hot water,' he smiled. 'Symbolic and so satisfying'

Chapter 30

'What happened next?' I asked.

As she always did, Saffron was giving me a run-down on her day at work.

'You know how this works, Oggie? We brought the suspect in for questioning,' she grinned. 'Dave was being his usual obstinate and argumentative self, if facts turned out not to match his preferred solution, but in the end the evidence spoke for itself.'

'And?' I asked, relieved it sounded like she wasn't having second thoughts on the DI Addison front after all.

'A result,' she gave a thumbs up and a satisfactory sigh. 'You see, the killings of Eve Fielding and Watson fell into the general category of 'reasons for murdering someone,' she explained. 'The obvious ones being 'power, money, and love' but in these cases add 'jealousy and ambition' to the list.'

'I'm just glad that's over,' stated my housemate.

'The killings aside, in Watson's case the additions of the severed foot and the scalding hot tub water, were meant to be symbolic or more like, shambolic,' Saffron was saying. 'Not sure why or what the clad foot in the shop window meant, probably the killer's warped sense of the dramatic. Anyway, Tristram Lang has been cautioned and charged with the murders of Eve Fielding and Colin Watson.

Tomorrow Addison is sending a team to the building site to investigate the plot number Lang gave us. With the help from Watson's builders, he's hoping they'll smash the concrete and find Eve's body. 'Cause, we only have Lang's word that she is buried where he says. The truth is, unless every block of concrete on every plot is destroyed, she may never be found.'

'So that's that then,' I said. 'Case solved, killer behind bars.'

Now I like to think I'm as intuitive as anyone and I sensed there was something, work related, still playing on her mind. Saffron was thoughtful and these days, a giveaway were the couple of frown lines anchored between her brows, seemed to be a permanent feature to her pretty face.

'What's the problem, Saff?' I asked.

Just like she was the only one I answered to, using an abbreviated version of my name, so my friend never objected if I shortened her name.

'This isn't over, Oggie,' she hugged one of the loose cushions, strewn along the length of the sofa.

(At this point, I have to state for the record, how much I hate those square, squishy monstrosities. When Saff's not about, I will endeavour to toss them to the floor before taking my rightful place. Just saying, that's all.)

'There is one crime, a possible murder which has been forgotten.'

Now at first, I struggled to see where this was going. To my experienced mind, the culprit had been apprehended and charged, and all was right in our detecting world.

'The team is slapping one another on their backs as a job well done. Down to the pub for a celebratory drink before putting up the

Christmas decoration in the morning,' she hesitated. 'I agree. A dangerous man is now about to stand trial in the new year, but I can find no reason or motive for the first foot found on the bin lorry. What about that crime? Everyone has overlooked it?'

I confessed I had, what with everything else going on.

'I hadn't forgotten,' she said. 'He was probably someone's son, brother, friend and they have as much right to know what became of him and find closure, as the Fieldings and Watsons of this world.'

Quite right too! I added for good measure.

Saffron continued. It's probably going to be my last case in this town, and I have a feeling any investigation off-the-grid is going to put someone's nose out of joint —.'

We both knew to whom she was referring.

'-- but in my spare time I'm going to follow up on the clues and whatever evidence we have.'

I knew that look of old: when my friend had a certain, determined expression on her face

– then the rest of the world should stand well clear.

'In the morning I'm going to ask for Aden Wright's help,' she added. 'He's got real potential in the police, if the rest would give him a chance and stop treating him like the office tea boy. He could reinterview the lorry crew and get a list of collections for that morning, if we assume the item was picked up on that earlier route and I'll chase up the lab results on the 'bin' trainer. I asked them a while ago to take another look at some of the trainer's ingrained dirt and stains. I know it was a long shot but I hoped there might be clues as to where the unknown male had been and, essentially, I could try to back-track his journey and maybe find out what happened to him.'

Good idea.

'What are your thoughts on us getting to the bottom of this?' Saffron asked for my opinion, as she always did.

'Way to go,' I answered.

Chapter 31

Constable Aden Wright was full of a sense that this assignment, solely and secretly given to him by DS Brook, was important work and nothing was too much for the smart, attractive sergeant. Of course, he'd heard the team's tasteless, and often, coarse remarks about the sergeant and the DI's affair, but he didn't take any notice of gossip.

He was still reliving the praise she'd recently heaped on him for finding the crucial CCTV footage which had subsequently led to closing the 'feet' cases. He'd do everything he could, starting with the bin men.

The young, eager officer was up and out even before dawn had broken on the freezing, winter's morning. He followed the council's gritter as it did its job, scattering sand and grit on the main road out of town. There were few other cars or vehicles at half past five on such a morning, but he wanted to be there, in plenty of time, to question Ted Lovell and the others before they set out on another day of emptying bins.

He was on a mission.

He located all four in the staff canteen and, as well as a bacon buttie and a large mug of 'builders', they treated him as if he was one of them.

'OK, lad,' said Gaffatape, Ted Lovell, the seasoned crew leader, chewing his way through a lovely, greasy English breakfast. In his opinion this was the only way to start his shift on such a freezing morning, knowing he'd probably suffer later with his troublesome ulcer.

'What is it you want to know we haven't already told you in our statements?' he asked.

'I'd almost forgotten about it, after all that's been going on,' stated Gary 'Just recently there's been feet found all over the place,' he spoke through a mouthful of nourishing porridge.

'Haven't they just arrested the bloke?'

'Ah,' grumbled Jim Howard. The gruesome find was something he'd rather forget. 'It gave me a fair old shock at the time, I can tell you.

You expect to find all sorts of muck in the bins, but not body parts.'

'I'd heard of other homeless people climbing into the backs of lorries for the night and then being trapped and crushed,' Bruce stared at his half-eaten food, and pushed the dish away.

It was noticeable that the young member, Toby Lee, stayed silent concentrating on his meal and listening to music on his earphones. He'd had enough grief from his cousin and cousin's mate's stunt, and he wasn't about to remind the rest of the crew, and get more of a 'ribbing'.

Constable Wright finished his mug of strong tea and cleared his throat. He pulled out the notebook and pen from his pocket and strove to appear professional. After all this was an important task given him by the detective sergeant.

He asked Lovell. 'On the morning you found the dismembered foot, can you remember your route? It was a Monday so was it the same each week?'

'Ah, every other Monday, every two weeks on that particular route covering the north side,' he paused and looked closely at the young officer seated opposite. 'But we told you all this a month or so ago.'

Word for word Aden Wright was writing it down in his neat handwriting, so he could relay the conversation to DS Brook later back at the police station.

'So there was nothing unusual or anything that roused your suspicions?'

'No nothing,' answered Gary Bruce. 'We emptied the bins along the streets and picked up the rubbish bags from the farms as usual. Same as we do week in week out.'

'So, if I can go over it once more,' he liked to be thorough, and was determined to impress DS Brook with his dedication to details.

Gaffatape was quite happy to tell it all over again: it was a viable excuse not to gather together his team and set out on another early start.

'Well let me see,' he said as he wiped the last of the egg yolk with the last piece of fried bread. The plate was virtually wiped clean.

'We must have left here around the usual time of six or thereabouts. As long as the job's done and the bins are emptied at the end of our shift, I'm not one to clock watch. First would have been the row of five isolated cottages a mile outside the town on the by-pass. Next through the countryside taking in a couple of farms. Then back into the town to the big estate, where most of our collection is done, and back to the tip and the depot in time for lunch.'

'So basic household rubbish, often in plastic bags, is emptied from the black bins straight into the back of the bin lorry? Where I assume it is crushed?'

'Ah, that's right. Each bin is loaded onto the hydraulic arm, then lifted and the rubbish tipped over the 'hopper' into the body of the truck where it's crushed by the compactor,' he recited the mechanics as if he'd learnt it from the manual.

'Once crushed it's then pushed to the end to make room for another load. Clever eh?'

'And every household has a black bin, right?'

'Right. The bins fit the lifting arm. Makes life easier for us. Except for many of the farms hereabouts when, quite often, the farmer will leave any of their household rubbish in large refuse bags for us to collect at the end of their farm tracks. Saves trying to get the lorry down the narrow tracks.'

Wright scribbled away.

'So,' he said, finally closing his notepad with all the details he could glean from the men. 'You are saying from the minute the empty lorry left the depot that morning to the discovery of the foot trapped in the mechanics in Morton Street, the item could have been in any of the rubbish bags collected on your way?'

'Ah, that's about right, lad.'

Chapter 32

'Yes, D.S. Brook,' said the woman on the other end of the telephone line. It was midmorning and, with the rest of the team fooling around, hanging tinsel and paper chains, resurrecting the forlorn-looking fake tree brought out for the sixth year and talking, excitedly, about a 'Secret Santa', DS Saffron Brook was at her desk phoning the lab.

'I have the results on the trainer, I was about to send it to your mailbox,' she continued without a pause.

'It's a cheap item, so no designer, limited edition or name of manufacturer, except for 'Made in China,' she reiterated.' Same as previous examinations. The pair would have been mass produced, possibly four or five years ago and sold in any of the online or retail clothing outlets. Well worn, they had almost certainly passed through numerous owners, before ending up on the victim's foot, so an absolute deluge of conflicting biological evidence. At a guess, latterly, they were a charitable handout from just about anywhere.'

That was exactly what Saffron had thought, but she was hoping for more.

'However,' continued the voice with an upbeat sound. 'As the victim apparently hadn't been wearing socks, inside the trainer I did find human skin tissue and DNA transferred from the foot. Unfortunately, there's no match on the database. The trainer itself has the usual dirt and grime and quite a number of different animal and bird faeces ingrained in the sole treads. Pigeon and dog, he could have picked up anywhere on the streets, and if the victim was from a town or city and homeless, plus the age and state of the trainer, that would make sense.'

She stopped talking to give the officer a chance to catch up.

'And,' she added as if leaving the best to the last. 'And – we swabbed the laces and found a minute trace of blood and something else, invisible to the naked eye it was almost missed. I thought it was most likely going to be the victim's, from when the foot was severed post-mortem.'

'A possible match to the perpetrator?' Saffron asked.

'Well, that was my initial thought but the 'something else' turns out to be *porcine scat.*'

'What's that?'

'Pig shit,' the voice said with immense conviction.

Chapter 33

'Now listen, Oggie.'

When Saffron used that tone, she meant business.

I listened.

'This is how I see it. From the lab results and then details of that particular morning's bin lorry collections, leads me to suspect the foot and trainer were, at some point, in or near to a pig farm.'

Right!

'There are four farms on the lorry's route. Two are arable farms meaning crops only, no livestock, and one does sometimes leave their household waste in bags to be collected by the lorry. The other arable farmer, very eco minded, recycles and composts everything. To my mind I think we can eliminate those two,' she was counting off on her fingers.

'Jacob's Farm, on the edge of the moorland, but is only a dairy farm so that can also be dismissed. Which leaves Fred Maynard, the place where all the fuss was with the climate activists in October. You remember it, Oggie?'

Oh yes, I do indeed. Rundown farmhouse with a couple of outbuildings surrounded by acres of fields, meadows, and land, ripe for building on, and bordered by the impressive ancient Woodpecker Woods. I recall the distant sight, and smell, of what some might term *a piggery,* but was just a large barn where Farmer Maynard bred pigs.

'Fred has a small herd if that's the correct collective noun for pigs?'

I didn't know, so couldn't comment.

'He slaughters and butchers the poor things for his own use, and sometimes sells pork and bacon products on a monthly-held farmers market.'

Here I have to insist I don't echo Saffron sentiments on eating meat: she is a vegetarian and I'm most definitely not.

'And,' she continued. 'Importantly, he does occasionally leave rubbish bags for collection at his gate. Lovell couldn't recall if they'd collected bags that morning, but thought it highly likely.'

She was silent and thoughtful. 'I just think it's odd if not a wild coincidence. It all began with that first foot in the trainer from an unknown source. We can ignore the second silly, boyish prank, and we now know the last two, Eve Fielding's and Colin Watson's were definitely connected, but does the link lead back to that first crime, I wonder?'

'Perhaps we should find out.' Was my suggestion.

'I've decided to take a drive out to Maynard's farm and have a word with the farmer and take a look round. I've left a message with Constable Wright to meet me there in an hour,' she added. 'You come too, Oggie. You may sniff out something I miss.'

I didn't need to be asked twice.

Close to, Maynard's Farm looked even more rundown and neglected than it had from a distance, the other side of the fields.

As we drove into the yard and, if we hadn't known different, would have imagined it abandoned.

DS Brook glanced around the area taking in the overgrown and weed filled small vegetable patch opposite the house that probably hadn't seen a carrot or potato in many a long year. Two forlorn barns, their large wooden doors hanging on by rusted hinges, faced the bleak farmhouse.

She knocked on the door and flakes of old paint drifted to the ground at her feet.

I waited as she knocked again then, with still no answer, took a step back to check the upper floor windows. No sign of the farmer or the usual farm dog or anyone living there. If Maynard was inside, he was ignoring his visitors.

Together we walked the perimeter of the building: the rear was as dilapidated as the front. Apart from a couple of empty and forgotten metal containers embedded into the overgrowth and a tall clump of nettles, there was little else in the grounds.

The other side of a bordering hawthorn bush, a vast field stretched away into the distance to the row of trees that indicated the boundary to Woodpecker Woods and where the protestors had camped a few weeks before. The area was now deserted, the tree branches finally cleared of their autumn colours.

From the *SOLD* board spiked into the ground and tipping drunkenly to one side, it was a sign the field had already been purchased for regeneration.

Had Fred Maynard already moved out?

I followed Saffron to the front and again she knocked on the door. Still no sign of life.

There should have been some sounds or smells, if only coming from the herd of pigs he supposedly kept close by.

Nothing! Not even the squawking from a crow in a nearby tree.

It was quite an eerie place and gave me the heebie-jeebies, my friend and police officer was made of sterner stuff.

We walked across the dirt strewn ground to the first barn. The door opened but the tired hinges squeaked their protest. The interior smelt of old: old wood, old diesel, old dust.

Side by side were a tractor, the tyres flat the vehicle unused for a season or more, and a car: from its relatively clean appearance still in regular use.

'So,' stated Saffron, running a finger along the dusty paintwork. 'Unless Maynard has another vehicle, he's probably close by.'

We walked the short distance to the twin barn and this time Saffron called out before trying the door.

'Mr Maynard. Fred Maynard. I'm with the police, Detective Sergeant Brook. Can I have a word–?'

The only sound in this strangely silent place was a plane suddenly flying overhead, so high it was leaving behind a vapour trail.

This time the inside, lit by a hole in a section of the roof and because half the far wall had collapsed, revealed old, musty bales of hay stacked haphazardly across the back. Apart from an array of old, broken farm implements and tools, there was nothing else. Loose dirt and straw littered the ground.

Except in here I was able to detect a sound through the gap, and coming from the west side of the land. It could have been the squealing of pigs somewhere in the far distance and located beyond the barns and the house, towards the edge of one of the fields. So Maynard did have animals, pigs, after all.

And they meant he was still here.

Chapter 34

We stood in the centre of the barn for a moment, so our eyes grew accustomed to the varying degrees of light. Outside the door the sky was already dulled by an advancing bank of clouds, so in the interior it was hard to make out shapes from shadows.

We walked across the floor to the hay bales, stacked into stepped formation. A few had already fallen, displacing others higher up.

The light caught and picked out a shining tube-shaped object nestling amongst the tangle of straw on a lower bale. Saffron leant forward to take a closer look, without actually picking it up. An empty and crushed soft drinks can and beside it, almost hidden by the strands of straw, a choc-bar wrapper. At first sight there was no knowing if these items had been there for months or a day.

'Looks like someone took shelter, and probably slept here,' said Saffron. 'Could it be—?'

A sound behind made me spin round to face the man, who had silently crept in through the open door.

'What d'you think you're doing in my barn?'

He was a heavily built man of average height. The semi-light told me he was ruddy faced with wisps of hair clinging to his balding head and along a jowly chin.

His top half was pushed forward so he gave an impression of suppressed anger and aggression, but this quickly accelerated when the pitchfork, held firmly in both hands, was suddenly aimed at us.

'I say again. What are you doing on my property?'

'Mr Maynard, I'm Detective Sergeant Brook,' answered Saffron showing her warrant card.

I wasn't a member of our wonderful police these days, so I didn't need an introduction.

I stayed silent, watching.

'I'd like to ask you about someone who I suspect was sleeping in your barn, possibly sometime in October. A young homeless man perhaps, who took shelter here?'

She indicated the items on the straw.

'Did you know he was here?'

Fred Maynard pushed his fleshy bottom lip over the top, as if working out how to answer.

'I know nothing. Now get off my land.'

'Did you think he was one of the protestors who were here back then?'

'I don't know what you're talking about. That lot of troublemakers didn't come 'til after–.'

'After what, Mr Maynard? After he stayed in your barn overnight or a few nights perhaps? You knew he was here didn't you?'

To my ears Saffron sounded confident and in charge and only her slight, nervous shaking, undetected by the man, gave away her true concern.

'No, I didn't. He was here in the morning, that's all.'

'So, what happened after you found him?'

He wasn't one of life's quick thinkers and he took a few minutes to answer, sensing he'd already given more away than he should.

'I didn't know who he was, just one of those 'traveller' sorts, you know?'

Saffron waited, while I stayed alert.

'He was wily, though. Thought he could get the better of me.'

The detective sergeant knew when to stay quiet, conscious that no one liked a long silent pause and soon felt the need to fill it. That included the Fred Maynard's of the world.

'We didn't know he'd been listening to our conversation. Sneaky like. Hiding behind the barn door when we were talking in the yard.'

'Who?'

'Doesn't matter who.'

We rightly guessed at the 'who' being Colin Watson, the property developer.

It was obvious Maynard was growing frustrated, by the way he clenched his teeth spitting out the words.

'The boy thought he could blackmail me when he heard talk of lots of money coming my way. He thought, because the payment was a backhander and probably illegal, he was entitled to a nice payday too. Well he was wrong.'

He stopped talking and, as if realising the enormity of what he just said, stared at the pitchfork still aimed in our direction.

She had come this far and Saffron had to know more, but I think she already had a vague idea. As did I.

'So instead of sharing your pay-out, you killed him?'

'No one takes what is mine,' it was an answer of sorts and spoken with building aggression.

'He shouldn't have been in my barn and he shouldn't have been listening in on a private conversation, and he had no right to demand money like that.'

'What did you do?'

'I told him I needed to think about it, and he should follow me indoors. I took him to the room at the back where I butcher the pigs,' for the first time there was a slither of a smile on his face.

'He wasn't keen on that. Didn't like the smell he said, and the thoughts of what happened to the beasts. I told him, killing is natural, a part of life.'

'You killed him there?'

He indicated the direction of the slaughter room by a nod of his head.

'Off the back kitchen, it was used as a large pantry when my folks were alive. Not much use for anything these days, except butchering pigs and greedy, demanding teenagers like that one.'

Chapter 35

The farmer felt no guilt, only justification for his crime, as he explained in a detached manner.

'I'm not sure the boy even saw death coming, before it was too late.'

He glanced at the fork, still held firmly between his hands, as if it was part of him.

'It was just a case of stripping off his clothes and cutting up his body into pieces to feed the pigs. Pigs will eat just about anything, but they're not partial to trainers. I burnt his clothes and one trainer, but I must have dropped the other trainer with the foot inside. Instead of starting another fire just for that, I added it to my household rubbish. I knew it would be collected the following Monday.'

'And you thought it would join the rest of the rubbish in bin bags and end up in the landfill?'

'That was the idea,' Maynard said.

Saffron was stating the obvious, but I sensed she was playing for time. Hadn't she said the constable was to follow us here. So where the hell was he?

As if reading her mind, Maynard shook his head with obvious delight. 'I know you came alone, I watched you from an upstairs landing.'

Nevertheless, he glanced back, beyond the open door and into the empty yard as if making sure.

Satisfied he turned back to face Saffron, and me, with renewed confidence.

'I've sold this dump and the land,' he said, relaxing and eager to tell us his good fortune. 'Just when I thought it had all gone wrong, what with the builder, Watson's murder, and the news over Councillor Fielding's bribery charges, up pops a better offer from one of the leading housebuilders. They didn't just want to buy the three fields Colin Watson was after, but have now bought the rest of the surrounding land with the farmhouse and all of the outbuildings.'

He licked his lips, savouring the telling.

'I felt like I'd won the lottery. Once the lawyers have settled everything and the money's in my bank, I'll have enough to start again and live the life I've always wanted.'

'You'll not get away with it,' said the sergeant, stating the much-used sentence and sounding quite determined but I knew Saffron, and she was not nearly as confident as she was sounding.

'My colleagues know where we are, and they should be here very soon —.'

He grinned and feint jabbing the fork in her direction.

'I don't think so, detective sergeant. I know you're bluffing, and no one knows you're here, or the cavalry would have arrived already. Now I need to finish off, clear up a few things, and I'll be spending Christmas and the New Year baking in the sun somewhere.'

'What are you going to —?' She didn't finish her question.

I'd been listening to what was turning out to be a dangerous situation and had worked out a plan. It might be a momentous moment and it could fail but, if I could wrestle the farmer to the ground, it may give Saffron time to escape. That was my thought process anyway, but no time to ponder the possible failure, it was time for me to act while his concentration was on my friend.

With speed that even surprised myself, I sprang at him.

I can remember hearing Saffron shouting my name as she realised what I was doing. It happened so fast and I suppose the outcome was inevitable, because at that precise second, Maynard turned the sharp, metal prongs of the fork towards me.

As the prong's pierced my side and I felt excruciating pain, I fell as the blood gushed from my wounds. I heard Saffron again, but I couldn't do anything to help her, as a mist drifted across my eyes.

I'd rather not dwell too long on those awful moments, only to add I thought we were both goners.

What followed, I found out later.

'What have you done?' Saffron cried. 'I need to help my friend — to stop the bleeding'? It was as much a plea, as an instruction.

Fred Maynard stared, his eyes un-focusing and bloodshot and, with added determination, turned the fork back to threaten DS Brook.

'I just need to finish you off and my pigs'll have the feast of their lives. Then it'll be time to get rid of all the evidence, and no one'll know you were here. Bit like that boy.'

He didn't sound sane.

'I'll then take care of the beasts before I'm on my way. Don't want to have Animal Rights complaining I neglected my pigs, now do I?' Another try at humour fell flat and he shrugged with little concern.

He jabbed again with the pitchfork and the prongs pieced Saffron's flesh. It was so sudden she didn't have time to cry out, let alone dodge his murderous attempt.

Maynard pulled back ready for a final time but, in my semi-conscious state, I thought I heard a sudden unmistakable sound like a 'clonk'. Was it metal against bone or, hopefully, a skull?

Chapter 36

Constable Aden Wright slammed his palms down on the car's steering wheel, with growing frustration.

He couldn't remember if DS Brook had actually stated a precise time, but she'd asked him to meet her at Maynard's Farm and he was on his way there now.

Or he would be if and when services cleared the road following a minor incident.

He'd already checked with the attending officers if anyone had been seriously hurt in the collision between a parked van and a driver who was starting his Christmas cheer early.

'No,' he was told by the officer. 'The car came off worse, with hardly a mark on the supermarket delivery. Both drivers are unhurt but the man driving the car had to be cut from his vehicle. He has already failed an alcohol test and been charged with drinking under the influence and reckless speeding in a built-up area. Unfortunately, the car was out-of-control, and hit with such force, parts of it are now obstructing the highway and will need to be cleared before we can let the traffic go.'

It was standard 'police speak' and as he was usually the one issuing such a statement Wright knew better than to argue.

He waited impatiently as the ambulances and police, and eventually the recovery vehicle departed, and the traffic could flow once again.

He drove as fast as he dared towards the farm, conscious of the other drivers on the roads, many who would be last-minute Christmas shopping. Once out, beyond suburbia and the town and into the open wildness of the countryside, he could speed up.

The light was fading, although it was only half past noon, and a weak, winter sun was already setting behind the line of trees making up the boundary between Woodpecker Woods and Maynard's Farm. Aden thought about driving the long way round, through the narrow, twisting lanes which would take him to the opening leading to the farm track, but reconsidered. He was already running late, no fault of his, but he didn't want to let the sergeant down. It might be best if he parked the car right here in this clearing, climbed over the fence, then *legged it* across the field to the farmhouse. Sprinting and running he was used to as he was a member of a local amateur athletic club and regularly raced in marathons. He reckoned he could do the distance in half the time it would take him to drive there.

Although it was much further than it looked from the line of trees, plus most of the ground was uneven, Aden still reached the yard in seven minutes.

The detective sergeant's car was parked to one side of the farmhouse fronting two large wooden and brick-built barns.

He followed the sounds of voices which took him past the first and to the second open door.

Aden peered cautiously in through the roof-height open door. A man had his back to him and was so intent on getting ready to attack the sergeant with the pitchfork, clasped tightly between two hands, he hadn't noticed the constable's arrival who, in the rapidly decreasing light could see Ogden, lying still on the floor. To one side Saffron swayed with blood oozing from the gash in her shoulder, hardly noticing the pain as she struggled to get closer to her friend.

The constable had to move fast, and with panic making his heart race, he searched for anything he could use as a weapon.

Resting against the wall, just inside the door, was a cast iron spade and holding his breath, he reached for it. Aden was fearful the man would sense him behind him, and Maynard was a big man, if it came to a fight, he didn't think he'd be able to overcome the farmer's strength.

The heavy solid oak handle felt rough in his hands as he firmly curled the fingers of both hands around the shaft, and steadied himself to take the weight.

They moved simultaneously. As Maynard pulled back the fork to thrust it into the terrified woman, the young constable lifted the spade above his head and brought business-end down on the farmer's head.

He dropped the fork, a look of shock and surprise on his face as if in slow motion, his knees gave way and he sank to the dirt floor.

Aden got ready to lift the spade and wallop the man again if he moved, but Maynard was out cold.

'Sarg,' he looked scared, as he rushed to her side.

Saffron was feeling faint with the loss of blood and shock, but she had to stay calm and in control.

'Phone for backup and ambulances,' she whispered, instructing the officer before she slid into unconsciousness beside Ogden.

Chapter 37

Well, that was more or less that.

Thankfully, our pitchfork wounds turned out to be flesh wounds, it was just so much blood that made them look fatal. It was thanks to our quick-thinking Aden Wright, the man of the moment, we weren't kebabbed.

Fred Maynard was arrested and, once checked over in hospital for possible brain damage: not likely with his thick skull, he was charged.

Not unsurprisingly the farmer had other plans. He denied killing anyone; after all there was no evidence and no body, so how could we prove anything? And he'd assumed we were trespassing in his barn and was only protecting his property.

In fact he decided he was innocent of everything and because he was now rich, thanks to the planning committee's decision to agree to the new housing on his land, he would be paying a top, London QC who, using a technicality, was likely to make him a free man.

Without proof it was Maynard's word against ours and for weeks we fumed together. How was it possible he could get off with cold blooded murder?

The three of us, Constable Wright, Saffron and I discussed this possibility.

'If only we could find out who that boy was, where he came from, find a link that would lead back to Maynard?'

I agreed. No body, and no real proof he was even in the area.

True, Forensic had had the unenviable task of meticulously going through the pig slurry, hoping to find traces of human remains.

Nothing. Nada!

'We have nothing,' said a frustrated Saffron. 'Except for the wrapper and the drinks carton, and even then, it could have been anyone bedding down in Maynard's barn for the night.'

'At least we have the killer of Eve Fielding and Colin Watson behind bars, and standing trial later next year. That was a result,' I offered hoping to make us feel better.

I'm not sure it did.

'The murder of the boy, whoever he was, may stay on the file,' said a determined Aden. 'But there's nothing to stop me from doing a spot of detecting in my own time.'

'Good for you,' Saffron said, not altogether enthusiastic, but ready to encourage.

'Good luck with that,' was my sentiment.

It could have turned out so much worse. Saffron and I could be dead, we were only seconds away from the killer thrust from the prongs on that pitchfork.

Now, as I nurse my wounds, trying hard not to pick off the remaining scabs, for idle entertainment I watch the lights on the tree in the corner switching, irritatingly, on and off in a rainbow of colours.

Saffron is busy alternating between watching yet another repeat of some boring film on TV, and packing some of the boxes ready for our move.

In a contemplative mood, I look back on the whole episode. The feet in shoes, three murders, sleaze, greed, love — it had it all, and of course I considered 'The Bizarre Case of the Severed Feet' could be a book, but that would be a project for M.J.C. Apparently she's an old hand at this writing malarky.

So, Christmas and New Year are over, and we look round our home for the last time. Tomorrow the removal van arrives, and we are off to our new home and new life.

My friend and housemate, the newly promoted Detective Inspector Saffron Brook, with Tomski the cat, and myself, we are off to start a new life in a rural town called Mulberry Hollow. I admit, with all these packed boxes, the general disruption, not to mention that daft cat, sensing the move, noting his travelling box waiting for him and doing a disappearing act, it's all very unsettling.

Saffron had been sprawling on the sofa, and seemed as 'flat' as I did. Outside the window of the house, in which she'd lived all her life, the day was calm, the sun bright in the surprisingly clear, vivid blue sky often present in mid-winter. Only yesterday she had commented on the first clump of snowdrops in the corner of the small garden, a sure sign spring wasn't far off.

She suddenly swung her legs off the sofa and stood, making me jump.

'I think we both need some exercise, Oggie,' she stated, stretching her recently injured shoulder as per Physio instructions.

'Let's make the most of this weather and stroll around this town for the last time.'

I couldn't have agreed more. I was up for that. Decision made.

'Right,' said my friend and housemate. 'While I get my coat, you fetch your lead.'

Those were words I always loved to hear, closely followed by:

'Ogden, let's go *walkies*.'…

Now which canine could resist that? …